SACRED FIRE

Visit us at www.boldstrokesbooks.com

SACRED FIRE

by
Tanai Walker

2014

ISBN 13: 978-1-62639-061-4

This Trade Paperback Original Is Published By
Bold Strokes Books, Inc.
P.O. Box 249
Valley Falls, NY 12185

First Edition: May 2014

Credits
Editor: Cindy Cresap
Production Design: Stacia Seaman
Cover Design by Sheri (graphicartist2020@hotmail.com)

Acknowledgments

Thanks to my GCLS mentors, Pol Robinson and Beth Mitchum, for taking the time out of their busy schedules to nurture a struggling writer. Also, thanks to Tammy for reading through one of my many drafts of this novel; you really helped me along. Thanks to Anders and Phair for the kick-in-the-ass crash course in writing they gave me one evening.

And a very special thanks to Radclyffe and Bold Strokes Books for all their help and support!

To Mom and Dad, who always knew I would be a published author someday. Thanks, Dad, for all your critiques and for being my very first editor. Thanks, Mom, for enabling my book habit and showing me how to look obsessively for a mix of beauty and order in the world. And thank you both for putting up with general weirdness throughout the years. You two are the best parents a writer could have.

CHAPTER ONE

My cell chirped and buzzed next to me on the passenger seat, letting me know I had received yet another text from Sandra. I glanced at the glowing screen as I parallel parked in front of a row of forgotten shops in a neglected part of town. I scanned the glass storefronts for some sort of clue of which door I was to enter. I put the car in park and checked my text messages.

Dinner?????

Her wordy attempts to engage me in an exchange of texts had diminished to one-word communiqués. I puzzled over the excess question marks, not quite versed in texting etiquette.

I sighed and decided to get back with her after my appointment. I stepped out of my car and into the stifling heat of a south Texas June. After a failed attempt to feed a broken meter, I wandered the strip that was partially shaded by torn and broken awnings.

The shop windows were all covered with tinting that was cracked and peeling away in big sections as if it had not been properly installed. I saw no sign of movement on the other side of the glass, only cluttered or darkened interiors. Beneath a sun-bleached but intact awning, I found a brass plate that read Cosmos' Antiques mounted on a narrow wooden door with a matching brass handle. I pushed the door open and heard the pleasant tinkle of a large antique brass shop bell. I looked up and smiled at its quaintness. Inside, long, heavy wooden tables covered with yellowed lace cloths were laid out with rows of tarnished silverware and china, stacks of books, and various odds and ends.

Cosmo waddled from the back, a tall, large man with heavy jowls and blond hair cut into a foppish bob that fell just past the top half of his ears. He smelled heavily of sage and wore a full black kimono with an ornate pink cherry blossom pattern. One of the sleeves was cut short to reveal a handless, deformed forearm that looked like a featherless wing.

"Tinsley Swan?"

"Hello, Cosmo."

He turned sideways to offer me his fully formed hand.

"I hope you'll join me for tea."

I agreed and Cosmo smiled as he swished past me, locked the door to the shop, and turned around the Closed sign.

"I apologize for the neighborhood," he said, motioning out the window. "Things are much different from when my mother first bought the place."

"Your mother owned this shop?"

"Yes, for over forty years, she sold antiques, mostly to other dealers with better clientele who no doubt marked them up, but Mother never minded. She always liked old things."

He motioned for me to follow him. We walked behind the glass counter dominated by an ancient cash register, to a sparsely decorated room. A large wooden desk squatted in one corner, and what I suspected was a cot stood folded in a narrow hall off to the side. Cosmo pulled out a chair for me at a small table. I sat before a bamboo mat set with Japanese tea bowls, teapot, a cauldron, and dipper.

A tea ceremony? Really? How strange.

"I hope you like matcha," Cosmo said.

"Of course."

"I so rarely have visitors of good taste," he said. "And when Jimmy said you would be stopping by, I began to prepare."

"You didn't have to go to so much trouble."

"I must disagree." He smiled and bowed his head.

How strange. I bowed and watched as he used tiny spoons to measure out powdered tea and spices into the two bowls. His movements were careful and deliberate. Cosmo used a bamboo ladle to measure out hot water and drop each serving into cups so that even the thin tendrils of steam rose uniformly. I found myself no longer uncomfortable but entranced.

He then placed one bowl inside a wooden container anchored to the table. I realized this was to hold the bowl steady so Cosmo could use his good hand to wield a short-handled bamboo whisk to beat the green tea mixture until a bit of foam rose to the top.

He removed the bowl from the container and turned it several times before he slowly slid it in front of me. Cosmo bowed and removed a cheesecloth from a plate of round cookies pressed with the shapes of Japanese characters. He whisked himself a bowl of tea and sat.

Cosmo smiled and waited until I lifted the bowl to my lips before he did.

"How wonderful," I remarked, surprised at the herby, refreshing taste with just a hint of spiciness, all enhanced by one of the little cookies. All of it left me remarkably calm, and I didn't feel so anxious about this precursor to the viewing of the merchandise he had to offer.

"I'm glad you approve," Cosmo said with a satisfied smile. "My brother is always boasting about how he contributes to your marvelous collection. I'm glad I can be of service to you. The antique business can be a lonely one."

"I never imagined," I said sympathetically, though I couldn't have cared less.

"If you're not well connected or in a trendy area of town," Cosmo said. "But you don't want to hear about my woes. You came here to see lovely things."

He slipped his hand under the bamboo mat and produced a black file folder, which he opened to reveal an ivory envelope. He handed it to me with the same sense of ceremony as the serving of the tea.

I took the envelope, opened it, and gently removed the contents—seven turn-of-the-century postcards in their own protective tinted Mylar pouches. My fingers trembled and my heart accelerated as I handled each one. They were of exquisite quality, and a few were definitely French.

All the postcards featured women in various poses and stages of undress, mostly black-and-whites with a few sepia tones. I looked up at Cosmo, who munched on a cookie nervously as he watched.

We both flushed.

"You like them. I can tell," he said quietly. "Would you like more light to view them?"

"I brought one," I said and removed a lighted magnifying glass from my satchel. I used my fingernail to gently open one of the pouches.

I slid the first postcard from its pouch and switched on the glass. It felt as if I were looking through time, back to these stoic, lush women with their smooth skin and fleshy hips. In all my years of collecting, I had never found one that lacked the element of cold, quiet beauty, even the more fetishist ones.

I eliminated two because they featured the same redundant pose of a nude girl, her back turned to the camera with one arm stretched up as she looked over her shoulder. Another I eliminated featured a "schoolroom" scene with a clothed "teacher" with a paddle and three "students" with their asses bared to the camera.

I found a definite keeper, the image of a woman reclining

nude in a wooden beach chair, a painted sea scene behind her. I liked the expression on her face and the singular curve of her body. There was another that caught my eye immediately. It was of a dark-haired woman, her head thrown back, one hand poised dramatically above her eyes, against her forehead, the other cupping one breast.

The fourth, I found oddly playful. There were two women on a love seat; one lay across the other's lap and waited patiently as the other cut the back of her undergarment with a large pair of scissors.

I gasped at the fifth when I saw a familiar face.

"I have this one, in a different pose and outfit, but I'm sure it's her."

Cosmo leaned across the table. "Really?"

I turned the card over and saw written in the upper left hand corner *To Charles from Malcolm.*

Charles just happened to be the name of my great-uncle. It was among his effects at my family's home in Galveston that I found the first postcards of my collection.

"It's the same background. I'm sure of it."

Suddenly light-headed, I studied the card. The familiar face of a young woman looked back at me. She reclined on a pile of pillows fully nude, her pubic area trimmed to match the V made by her thighs and sex. One arm was raised over her head, and her legs were crossed at the calf, one foot arched, the toes pointed. The entire effect gave the appearance that she was in the middle of a stretch. Her large, heavy-lidded eyes looked drowsy as if she had awoken from a catnap to have her picture taken.

"Lovely," I said and showed Cosmo. He seemed more interested that the photograph pleased me than in its subject matter.

I returned the pictures to their pouches, separated the four I wanted, and waited for Cosmo to name a price.

He made more tea instead, his ceremony just as precise. I accepted the second cup and sipped it to be polite, my mind on the pictures, especially the reclining woman.

Como smiled and began to make small talk.

"How long have you been collecting?"

The question annoyed me, but I answered it anyway. "Since I was fourteen."

"Fourteen. So young?"

I hesitated, mentally edited the story, and fast-forwarded past the summer of '83 and my visit to Salacia, and my run-in with a curse. It was better for me to forget that summer and to pretend the place never existed.

"Oh, you can tell me," Cosmo said and raised his good hand in a scout's honor.

I took a breath to steady my nerves. "The first ones were among some antique medical illustrations." That was partially true. I had only really started collecting the postcards after coming across them in an old bookshop when I was in my twenties.

"I really must get back. I'm expected for dinner." I was glad to have the excuse, even though I planned to get out of that engagement.

"And I'm going on like there's no tomorrow," he said. "I'll let them go for eighty-five, no, seventy-five each."

"Eighty-five each is fine."

"But you came such a long way," he insisted.

"If I got a bargain on these, it wouldn't be any fun."

He laughed. "I suppose you're right."

I opened my checkbook, pen poised. "Do you perhaps have any type of small accessory for a woman?"

"I have lots of things. Is it for you?"

"No, it's an appreciation gift for my boss. She's into, you know, Chanel and Louis whoever. I was thinking of a brooch, perhaps."

"Or a cameo." Cosmo grinned and stood. "I have just the thing."

I followed him to the front of the store. He showed me a row of cameos inside the glass counter. They certainly looked like "just the thing," and way more than I cared to pay for a gift for Sandra.

"Don't worry. These are reproductions from the sixties. They're more vintage than antique," he said and presented me with one of a partially veiled woman with a serene, almost Madonna-like expression on her face.

"It's resin, not shell, but it's trimmed in sterling silver with a turquoise background," Cosmo said. "Your boss will certainly be impressed with your good taste."

I pondered the gift for a minute. It was the first in our very short courtship and would make it harder to get rid of her. The cameo would make her smile, I was sure of it, and that gave me a thrill. I sighed. Why did fucking someone make you want to buy gifts?

Cosmo grinned, thinking the price of the purchase gave me pause.

"I'm sure we can make a deal."

❖

I decided to go to dinner with Sandra after all. I would give her the cameo and take her home to my bed. In less than a week, I would have to disappear off the face of the earth for seven days. I would have to break things off. Yes, it was an asshole move. Yes, there would be a special place in hell for me, but not just because I ended a short-lived affair with Sandra Ortega.

I made my way home blasting my AC to ward off the triple-digit heat. As I turned down my street, the Volvo's tires made a pleasant hum against the cracked and uneven one-hundred-year-old red bricks that paved Valentine Lane. My street was one of several forgotten by the city when it upgraded to cement, just as it had been forgotten when the city first covered the dirt roads with bricks.

At the end of Civil War, ex-slaves claimed the area and established a community with its own schools, a hospital, stores, and churches. They named it Freedman's Town, and like such neighborhoods across the country, it became a haven from the Jim Crow madness of the South. The first residents of my neighborhood purchased the bricks for the roads themselves and laid them. These days, dilapidated houses, and churches over a century old stood cheek and jowl with newly built, stylish townhomes. In a city that longed to take its place among the country's magazine-named ranks of the best cities to live, history stood in the path of progress.

Sixteen years ago, I saw a different opportunity for sanctuary when I heard about the uproar over a brick Baptist church that was to be torn down, the land it had sat on since 1896 sold to the highest bidder. The new owner of that lot happened to be my father, who was not too thrilled at being the center of such a scandal. I talked him out of the land for a reasonable price, and renovated the church into a house.

Eventually, the housing market bombed and an inevitable recession followed. The revitalization of Freedman's Town stalled with only the outer perimeter finished with a high-rise of lofts, a few sidewalk cafés, fine restaurants, and trendy businesses. Meanwhile, the center of the neighborhood continued to crumble around the new houses and their yuppie residents.

My home remained, hidden in the center behind a massive, even older Baptist church and two cemeteries. I despised elitist yuppie neighborhoods. While my more professional neighbors anxiously awaited signs of continued development, I lived in complete contentment.

A group of kids huddled together at the curb in front of my house, their heads bent as they inspected something in the street. Several rusted, scraped-up bikes blocked my driveway.

I stopped and gave my horn a quick bleat, but the children didn't seem to notice. They were the children of the row houses, and they had the run of the neighborhood during the summertime.

I inched the Volvo closer and honked. Several of the group of about six looked up at me and then turned their attention to the street before them. I climbed out of the car to see what was going on.

They took notice of me and seemed to snap out of their trance. The children ranged in ages from about five to nine, boys and one girl. They were dressed in an assortment of shorts, jeans, and T-shirts. What they did all have in common were black armbands silk-screened with some logo of a rising sun that doubled as the face of a lion.

I saw what they were huddled over: the carcass of a possum, buzzing in the summer heat with several species of fly. The smell nearly knocked me out, yet it also fascinated me. My stomach rumbled, not with disgust but hunger. I backed away a few steps, shocked at the reaction.

One of the kids studied me with large, soulful eyes. He had dusky skin and a cap of sleek black hair. Perspiration beaded his face.

"It's a dead cat-snake," he said solemnly.

I frowned in disbelief of their ignorance. "That's a possum. You kids shouldn't bother with it. You could catch a disease."

A few of them stepped back, alarmed.

The only girl among them looked up and scowled. "She's lying. People can't get no animal diseases."

Before I could open my mouth to object, one of the kids pulled the neckline of his T-shirt over his nose.

"H-One N-One," he shouted.

The other kids stepped back, shrieking, "Swine flu, swine flu. Cooties."

I followed suit, alarmed at their sudden clamor. The girl retreated reluctantly. Still scowling, she removed a deck of cards with the same sun lion logo from her pocket. The girl flipped through the deck and removed a card, then tossed it onto the dead possum. The flies hovered above the carrion in a dense, humming cloud. Curious, I peered down at the picture on the card. It glittered with stars and read: Soul-Recycle! Transmorphation!

"What is that?" I asked.

"It's a Sun-Monster card. It's a death card so the Snake Cat can come back as Viper Cat."

"Viper Cat," some of the other kids echoed.

"How strange," I said under my breath as they gathered themselves and their bikes. I began to walk back to the car. The soulful-eyed kid circled me on a mountain bike way too big for him. He stretched out one arm toward me. In his hand, between two fingers, he held another one of the colorful cards.

"Take it," he said.

I hesitated.

"Take it," he insisted. "Go on."

I took the card and studied the graphic. It featured a lanky, brown-skinned man in a lab coat, with a rooster-red pompadour coiffed into a single red curl over his forehead. He had one eyebrow cocked, and round spectacles perched on the end of his nose. He could have been my anime caricature.

I grinned despite myself.

"It's Professor Swiggleslock," the boy said. "His specialty is alchemy."

"Alchemy?" I laughed. "How does a little thing like you know about alchemy?"

"He changes the monster's elements," the kid said as he pedaled away fast to catch up with his friends.

I climbed back into the Volvo, tossed the card onto the dashboard, and used the remote to open the gate and garage. The door rolled down behind the car and shut out the bright light of the day. It was good to be home, in my dark, quiet, stuffy garage. I slipped out of the car and quickly gathered my suitcase and carryall from the trunk.

I walked the short, covered breezeway that connected the house to the garage and let myself into the kitchen. I tossed my keys on the counter, and tapped the code into the pad for the alarm system. Beyond the kitchen was once the vestibule—now the living room—where the congregation once sat in their oiled wooden pews. I had restored one of the pews myself, and it sat against a wall near the front door.

A staircase led to the second floor. A short hallway led to my bedroom, bath, and my office. I parked my suitcase in the hall and took my carryall to my office, the largest room on the second floor. The desk where I kept my workstation was a stainless steel, L-shaped behemoth I admired in the showroom for its efficient look, but hated once I got it home. Half the desk was designated for sketching, the other half for three panels of computer monitors and two PC towers.

There was still plenty of time left for a little alone time before giving Sandra a call. I removed the new postcards from my satchel and scanned them into digital copies to be saved on a memory stick. The originals would go with the others, locked in a small antique rolltop desk. Before stashing them away, I lined them up on the desktop like a child introducing old dolls to new ones.

The first of the postcards I had ever acquired, the pride of my collection, featured a woman who looked to be dressed in a shining Egyptian-styled costume. A gauzy skirt hugged her hips; the sheer fabric revealed her sex between parted thighs. A metallic-looking girdle began at her midriff and stopped below her bare breasts. On her head rested a massive headdress that circled her face like a halo, with horns protruding from the sides. She wore shining plates on her shoulders and an array of bangles and bracelets on her outstretched arms. One hand held a crop, the other a flail.

I called her the Golden Goddess.

When I was a teenager, I found the photograph and two others of the same woman inside a copy of *Justine* by the Marquis de Sade. Since that summer, I have studied the images and wondered who she was and why I have been looking for her in all the others I have collected. My fingers trembling as if I was fourteen again, I took the Golden Goddess and the reclining girl purchased from Cosmo to my sketching area. I turned on the lamp and lay them side by side.

The same heavy-lidded eyes stared back at me from both photographs, seeming to challenge comparison. Their secret half-smiles were identical, so slight they seemed to be water-colored on in some clever turn-of-the-century photo editing. The breasts were small and pert, the nipples dark.

The same girl.

I went to the rolltop and put the pictures away. The desk looked like it would be hard to move, but there were wheels hidden beneath. I easily pushed it away from the wall and removed the framed Kalmakov print of his interpretation of Astarte. The wall there was blank save the outline of a door. I pushed the left side of the panel, and it turned to reveal a small room. A motion-sensor fluorescent light flickered on.

The room was a ten- by ten-foot cell with a floor and padded white walls. A small table and chair waited in the center of the room. On the table sat a black projector and a laptop. I booted up the computer and projector and ported the memory stick. I activated a screen to slide from a compartment mounted to the ceiling. With the push of another button, the lights dimmed. From speakers mounted on the walls a selection from a local string quartet began to play its dark, moody music. I settled into the chair.

The slideshow started. My face flushed hot from the usual pangs of shame. This was my sanctuary. Nothing could touch me here. I unbuttoned the fly of my jeans and slipped my hand between my thighs, beneath my underwear. I kicked off my shoes, as they felt tight and uncomfortable suddenly. As the postcards flashed on the big screen, I visited with each of them, one at a time, the girls I had collected over the years, staring at me through time. My Golden Goddess appeared, her arms stretched out, with her crop and flail.

The music reached its crescendo, and I followed soon after. The slide show ended with the Golden Goddess without her regalia, reclined on cushions. Perfection. I gazed at her until the screen went black, her image burned as a negative afterimage into my eyes. My heart hammered in my chest, and I attributed it to the excitement of my activities. I sat up and took a few deep breaths. Though the room was cooled by several vents, sweat dripped from my temples, and the wetness in my pants increased with sweat. I straightened in my chair, and a wave of pain bent me over. Every muscle in my body seemed to spasm at once, while my bones trembled as if threatening to leave my body.

I cried out and eased myself to the floor.

The change. The curse.

It could not be. The beast had never manifested itself until midnight of the seventh day of the seventh month of the seventh year. Then again, how could anything so strange and otherworldly be on a fixed schedule?

The pain receded slowly. The power of it always took me by surprise. The worst part was the fleeing of my consciousness like black water down a drain. It didn't happen this time, and I hoped that it meant the change wouldn't come until its appointed time.

I began to stand slowly, not sure of my balance. Halfway up,

I happened to look down at my feet. The sight turned my legs to rubber, and I fell on my ass.

Just below my toes, two thick patches of coppery hair had grown on the tops of my feet. I gasped and shook them briskly as if the hair would just fall away. I folded my leg to examine the new growth and found it coarse and bristly. I tugged at it a bit and sucked in air at the pain.

"Oh shit, oh shit," I muttered and began to pace the small area. I could never get used to the transformation. That year made my fifth cycle, the third here in the safety of my house, locked in the hideaway room for seven days and seven nights, hardly conscious of anything but a clinging, desperate loneliness.

I left my padded room and replaced the desk and the Kalmakov print. In the rolltop, I kept my journal. The book didn't document my daily life, but the cycle I had been cursed with since the age of fourteen. The last entry was dated nearly seven years before, July fifteenth.

> *The dreaded seven days has come and gone once again. As usual, there is little memory of the previous week past the moment I locked myself in. A close call this time. The change came upon me fast on the evening of the sixth. Barely made it to the safe room. I do not know who to thank that it held. I feel tired and achy and may take an extra day from work to recover.*

I read back to my second cycle, when I decided to document the change. The first page of the book was titled "Signs." It was a list of symptoms that preceded the change.

Nausea
Racing pulse
Slight fever—worsened as transformation day
   approached

Heightened sense of smell
Pain in joints and muscles
Fatty food cravings (body fat greatly reduced before
    and during transformation)
Strange impulses

I thought of Sandra. As much as I wanted to see her, I was too rattled to be of much company. Then there was the risk. I padded out of the room to find my phone. There was no text message from her, so I sent one of my own.

Can't do dinner. Not feeling well. Sorry. See you Monday.

She answered right away: *Whoa, that was sudden. I'm beginning to think you're avoiding me.*

I texted back: *Of course not.*

I paced around the room until my phone chirped again.

You're full of it Tinsley Swan. See you Monday.

For once, I wished that I were, that I could go out to dinner with her and bring her home to stay the night. Hell, she could stay forever if her presence would ward off the beast. But I could never have that. I could take lovers in between the cycles, but there was always the fear I would meet one and not want to let go, that I would attempt to lie to her on that seventh week of that seventh month of that seventh year. There was the chance the beast would come and devour some poor woman in the night, leaving me in a bloody bed to sort it all out.

I turned my attention to my feet and let out a dry laugh of relief. The patches of hair had vanished just as mysteriously as they appeared. After inspecting my feet closely, I put my shoes back on. None of this mattered. Soon, the change would take over me, as it would every seven years for the rest of my life.

CHAPTER TWO

For the remainder of the weekend, I stayed cloistered in my home, close to my secret room, just in case the beast returned. I felt tired, achy, and restless. After a nearly sleepless Sunday night plagued by dreams I did not remember, I woke feeling somewhat myself.

Usually, working from home was no problem, but the medical illustration studio I worked for had recently been swallowed up by a larger firm. Being the longest tenured employee, corporate handed down an art director title, which meant longer hours and less time in my home office. Grateful not to be in my early forties and searching for a job in this economy, I complied.

Armed with a thermos of strong tea, I made my way straight to the conference room for a nine a.m. meeting, the first since the finalization of the acquisition of Zidonis Medical Publishing by OddDuck Studios.

I said hello to everyone and took my seat on the right side of the long mahogany table, and quietly sipped my tea as I listened to the creatives and the executives talk about their weekends. There were three of us salvaged from Zidonis, me and two guys, both named Bill.

The rest of them were OddDuck people, young, hip, and chatty. They were the types who went to music festivals to see obscure bands and attended food truck tastings. I cooked at home to avoid eating out alone, while the Bills were both married with college kids.

I shifted in my seat. Someone was wearing way too much aftershave, an oppressively masculine scent that made my eyes water slightly. I straightened and rolled a foot away from the conference table, slowly, so no one would notice. I glanced around the room at the faces of my colleagues. None of them seemed to be bothered.

"Sandra's late," someone remarked.

I gulped down my tea and considered stepping out for a brief breath of fresh air. A tug at my elbow, and I turned to face Bill Macy, who grinned wryly.

"You don't look so hot, Swan."

I wanted to tell him that I didn't feel so hot when a new smell assaulted my nostrils. It was the moist smell of decay as if Bill Macy had eaten roadkill for breakfast.

On the other side of me, the other Bill, Bill Sands, whispered conspiratorially, "Hit the bottle too hard last night, Tinsley?"

I smelled alcohol-tinged sweat and whiskey fumes. Someone had indeed imbibed, and Bill and I both knew it hadn't been me.

"I'm fine," I managed, but the smells were multiplying like a chorus of whispers. Coffee, hair products, leather, polished wood, ink, starch. The beast had come through without so much as a warning pang to share its sense of smell. I stiffened in my chair, prepared to bolt at the first sign of the beast's physical approach. In seconds, I felt dizzy to the point of lip-numbing nausea. A dull throb bloomed from a bud of sharp pain behind my ear and slowly claimed my sinus cavity and right eye.

Then Sandra Ortega, creative director of OddDuck's brand-new Houston studio, stepped into the room. She wore a short-sleeve pearl-colored dress that twisted at the neck and hung lower on the right side, revealing her delicate collarbone. Her honey-brown hair, expertly highlighted with blond streaks, hung between her shoulder blades in a ponytail. She brought with her the smell of good, subtle things like fruit and flowers and face powder. She scanned the room, her eyes falling on me last.

"Good," she said blandly. "Everyone's here."

A murmur of good mornings echoed throughout the room, and my new boss, and lover, waved them away as she sat at the head of the conference table while she finished a text message on her smartphone. Her scents gathered around her like an aura. I tried to focus on them, ground myself in them. I thought of watching her asleep in my arms. My heart began to hammer in my chest, and suddenly, it was too hot in the room.

Sandra raised her head and flashed everyone a perfectly capped smile. She spoke with a smoky, sugary South Texas drawl that could cajole or cut like a knife.

"What have we got, people?"

One of the younger designers pointed a remote control at a projector mounted to the ceiling and flicked off the lights. When he passed me, the smell of sickish sweat trailed behind him, breaking my focus on Sandra. My only line of defense crumbled to bits, and the world seemed to cave in on me in the form of scents.

A screen glowed blue on the opposite wall. The illustrated image appeared: a caduceus with two serpentine ducks wrapped around the staff in the place of snakes. The words OddDuck Medical Multimedia swirled around the new logo.

Everyone applauded halfheartedly. The young man looked pleased with himself. There were more slides and talking. I hardly heard any of it. My head throbbed, and it felt as if all the smells would strangle me.

I stood slowly, determined to make my exit as smooth as possible. The light in the hall nearly blinded me, and I stumbled forward to the nearest ladies' room.

It was blessedly immaculate and silent of any activity. I went for the sink and turned on the cold tap. I bathed my hands, dashed two palmfuls of cold water on my face, and watched my dripping, panting reflection in the mirror. I felt drained. My skin, usually the color of toasted ginger, looked more like blanched almonds. I slowly sighed out a breath, and inhaled.

A familiar pain streaked from the base of my spine to the base of my neck, and the throb in my head accelerated. My ribs buckled inside my chest and rippled at my back. A moan escaped my throat and echoed off the tiled walls and floor.

I felt my shirt tighten around me, the collar constrict around my throat. With a fumbling hand, I tugged at the fabric. A button popped against the mirror and ricocheted onto the counter.

My knees buckled, and I leaned on the sink to keep my balance, gripping the rim with hands stiffened into claws from the agony.

The beast was coming, and I was nowhere near home and my secret room. I needed to hide. I let go of the sink and crawled backward to the stall behind me. I managed to prop myself onto the toilet and lift one cramped leg to close the door.

My panting came quicker now, and I was burning up with fever. The leather of my loafers began to creak with strain. I slipped my feet free. They had sprouted copper hair, the same shade as that on my head. Curved black claws grew before my eyes. I checked my hands to find them in the same state. Hair peeked from my cuffs.

The hinges on the restroom door squeaked. I held in my short, shallow breaths and waited.

High-heeled shoes clip-clopped toward the stall where I sat. The heels were on the feet of familiar caramel-colored legs.

"Tinsley Swan," she said. "If you weren't feeling well, you should have stayed at home." She stopped before the stall. "Are you dead in there?"

I felt pretty damned close. I opened my mouth to speak, to tell her I was fine and she should go back to the meeting if it wasn't over. A raspy growl came out instead of words.

"Tinsley?" Sandra asked. "Why are your shoes off? Tinsley?"

She could not find me like this, her lover, a hideous beast.

"Go."

I was barely able to form the word, and it sounded more like a bark. I tried again.

"Go."

The stall door swung open, and there stood Sandra clutching her smartphone. Her eyes widened when she saw me, her jaw hung open, and a bleat of terror rang out from her tanned throat.

She slapped her hand over her mouth and stared for a moment. I was helpless under her scrutiny. Frozen.

She kneeled next to me, on the ladies' room floor, in her white dress. Her phone fell to the tiles with a clatter. Her hand left her mouth, and she whispered my name, then used the hand that stifled her scream to touch my leg. I jumped. Sandra gasped, startled.

I glanced up, past her, to the mirror beyond the open stall door. I saw my face, long and gaunt, my hair a bushy red mane. Seven short, crooked black horns protruded from my forehead, temples, and crown.

"My God," Sandra whispered. "What are you?"

Was it not obvious to her? I was a monster, something she should run from, call some sort of authorities to come and put me out of my misery. It was one of my biggest fears, beasting out and running amok around the city. The whole scenario ended with me being shot down in the street like a rabid dog.

The pains came again, and the edges of my vision blurred. I felt my body tilt over, my head hit the stall wall with a thunk. I felt Sandra's arms around me, lifting me back into a sitting position. I opened my eyes to see her looking at me.

"You're back," she said softly.

I groaned in reply.

"Jesus. Do you need to go to the hospital or something?" she asked.

"Certainly not," I managed, my voice a tortured whisper.

She straightened. "What the hell was that?"

"Nothing."

Sandra frowned. "It didn't look like nothing. You changed."

I rolled my eyes and tried to sit up on my own. A wave of dizziness kept me slumped on the toilet. "You were not supposed to see that."

A pounding on the outer door startled us. A male voice inquired about me.

"She's fine," Sandra said, her eyes on me. "Low blood sugar."

We sat in silence for a moment. She leaned forward. "You're going to tell me everything—"

"Or else what?" I countered. "You're going to tell everyone my secret?"

She let out a sarcastic chuckle. "I just might."

I felt my lips pull into a trembling smile.

Sandra disappeared from my view, and I could hear the paper towel dispenser going. She reappeared at the sink with a wad of paper, which she carefully wet in the sink. She returned to me and carefully dampened my face. After a few minutes, she leaned back, inspecting me.

"Not a mark," she said, brushing my forehead with her fingers. I grabbed her hand and pulled it away.

"You should forget what you saw."

She shook her head. "Not in a million years."

I slipped my shoes on, and she helped me to my feet. We walked slowly out of the ladies' room to my office. I collapsed in my chair behind my desk and watched Sandra pace my office, texting someone. When she was finished, she looked over at me and waved a manicured hand.

"Is that why you couldn't see me Friday night?"

I nodded.

"Well, that explains a whole lot."

"Like what?" I asked, though I knew what she was talking about.

"Why you're so damned unavailable, why you have your walls up so high." She sat across from me. "So how long has this been happening? What is it exactly?" She leaned over the desk. "Are you a werewolf?"

I chuckled, despite myself, at all the questions. "No. I'm not a werewolf."

She leaned forward. "So? Tell me."

"Sandra, I shouldn't involve you in this. It could be dangerous for you, especially now. Things are stranger than usual for me."

"What do you mean stranger than usual?" she asked.

I sighed in defeat. "I only change for seven days, every seven years on the seventh day of the seventh month." I looked at her pointedly. "Never a minute sooner."

She straightened. "Wow. What do you do for those seven days?"

"I hole up in my house. I have a special room I lock myself in."

"And then?" she asked. "You just prowl around in there? Are you conscious of yourself? I mean, does your mind change?" I messaged my temples. "I remain somewhat conscious, like when you're dreaming and you know it. Yes. It's like a very long, troubling sleep."

She winced sympathetically as she stood. She walked around the desk and behind my chair. Her hands landed on my shoulders and she began to rub them, her thumbs playing alongside my spine. Sandra's proximity made me nervous, and I looked to see if the door was closed. It was.

"Don't worry," she said softly. "You're not well, so I'm helping you."

I scoffed. "By giving me a backrub?"

She shushed me.

So I did. After a few minutes under her attentions, I felt my aches and pain fade in the wake of a pleasant tingle in my ribs, a total opposite feeling of the agony of the change.

"You know if anyone sees this, it will ruin your rep," I said.

"Well, I'll say I forced you."

I wondered why she hadn't run, why she wasn't afraid. The tenderness brought tears to my eyes, and I quickly blinked them away.

"Thank you," I managed to say. "I feel much better now."

"Do you want to go home?"

"No," I said. "I have that liver model to work on."

She stepped around the chair to face me. "Take it easy, then. If you feel weird—"

"I'll be fine."

She smiled. "We're having dinner tonight, so don't try to get out of it. You owe me a hell of a story."

I sighed. "As long as we stay in."

She grinned wryly. "Your place or mine?"

I narrowed me eyes. "Mine. You bring the dinner."

"One massage and you're ordering me around?" She sauntered to the door, opened it, and paused to look over her shoulder at me.

"Take it easy."

When she was gone, I slumped in my seat. It seemed every bone in my body protested at even the slightest move. Perhaps as I got older, the change would take more of a toll on me. It made sense. Sandra's touch had been like a balm.

She certainly had a way about her. When she first arrived in Houston, I found her pretentious and abrasive, yet attractive and witty, a breath of fresh air after working for years with the same stale white men. Then there was the Dallas trip to finalize the acquisition of Zidonis. Sandra and I started drinking at the bar in the hotel where we were staying.

We talked of work and the music we liked. She told me she thought I was talented, and sexy. I didn't have much to say after that and followed her, docile as a lamb, to her room, where more cocktails were consumed.

During the course of the evening, I became aware of several things: she had nice legs, even nicer skin, and she was moving closer and closer to me. I did nothing to widen the space between us. Desire hung in the air, the moment when two people come to the unspoken agreement that they're going to spend the night together. We kissed and she moved away, taking off her clothes and revealing a body more tantalizing than the black-and-white Golden Goddess I had gazed at for so many years. She returned to me, warm and alive. We made love and she slept in my arms.

I sighed at the memory, as I had during the two weeks since our first encounter. I had tried to avoid Sandra like the plague. Now she knew my secret. She hadn't run away screaming. She had stayed and given me a shoulder rub.

❖

Sandra arrived at my place by seven. By then, I had showered, napped, and re-groomed. I opened my gate with the remote and waited for Sandra's car to enter. Through her windshield, I could see that she was making an exaggerated face of surprise.

"*This* is your house?" she asked as she exited the car with two large brown paper bags.

I went to help with her burdens.

"It's a fortress," she said as she squinted up at the peaked roof, below the crest. A cross of lighter-colored brick contrasted with the darker brick of the rest of the house.

"I planned it myself," I told her.

I led her to the front door for the grand tour.

Sandra looked at the high wooden eaves over the foyer, then at me, as if she saw me in a different light. "This is fucking unbelievable."

"It spoke to me."

"I never imagined you living in an old church," she said as we moved to the kitchen. She began to unpack her bags of savory-smelling plastic-covered foil containers.

"I brought mole," she said.

At my questioning look, she opened one of the containers to reveal various chicken parts smothered in a thick, dark sauce. In the others were rice, beans swimming in broth, and corn tortillas.

I had a bottle of sangria on hand. I opened it while she set the table. The scene of domesticity was not lost on me. Would it be so bad to have someone by my side who shared my secret?

I turned to her. "This is a lot, Sandra. What I have to tell you."

She sighed. "I figured that, Tinsley, and I've heard some crazy stories in my time. I've lived some of them myself."

I frowned. "Nothing like this."

"You're afraid to tell me," she said. "You don't want to let me in, even though I saw you in beast mode this morning."

"So?" I asked. "What if I'm in league with the devil or something?"

She winced. "I hadn't thought of that. I don't see you as being one of the devil's minions. Are you? Because my people are staunch Catholics. They might disown me."

I narrowed my eyes at her. "You're making fun."

She laughed and we sat and dug into the sweet-spicy meal, at least I did. I polished off three pieces of chicken down to glistening bone in what must have been record time. I caught Sandra watching me and slowed down a bit.

"So where should I start?" I asked.

She raised her eyebrows. "Try the beginning."

I laughed. "Okay. About three hundred years ago, my ancestor, Alexandrine D'Orleans, started a secret cult of women based on Greco-Roman mystery cults. The center of their worship was something called Sacred Fire."

My mind flashed to that summer in 1983 and the Great Pyre, burning as tall as the Southern manor behind it. I saw Juliette, dancing the Dance of Seven Veils, her silhouette wreathed in glimmering flames.

Sandra took my hand, and for the second time that day, I was grateful for her comfort, still wary, but grateful nonetheless.

"I saw it one time, the Sacred Fire," I explained. "It looked like any bonfire, but there were faces in it, and instead of the crackle and roar of a fire, there were whispers."

Sandra shivered visibly. "What happened?"

"My aunt, Quinn Tinsley, initiated me when I was fourteen. My mother took me to Galveston, her family's home Salacia, just miles from the spot where Alexandrine landed, bringing her cult to the New World."

I poured myself another glass of sangria, remembering as I told the story for the first time since I testified against my aunt and the Sisterhood in court.

"They told me it was a secret society that had survived the ages, that there was a great power in my blood. The first ritual was the tattoo."

Sandra looked shocked, her eyes drifting to the area just above my right breast. The first night we slept together, I had lied and told her I got it during college. When she asked if it hurt, I told her no.

"It's more of a brand," I said. "Every seven years, the Sisterhood lights the Great Pyre to bring the Sacred Fire. They save the last fire's embers in a special box. They burned the seven-sided star into my skin using the embers."

"The fuck." Sandra stood. "Are you telling me that it's not a normal ink tattoo?"

"No. It's not." I downed my sangria. I was going to need something stronger. I went to the refrigerator where I keep a bottle of Old Raj gin.

"So what was the next ritual?"

"Oh," I said, preoccupied with fixing myself an after-dinner martini. "They put the mask on me. I saw terrible things."

"Do you have it?" Sandra asked.

The bottle of gin slipped out of my hand. I managed to catch it between my hip and the cabinet. I looked up at Sandra once it was secured.

"Hell no. I do not have the mask. I never want to lay eyes on that thing again."

I thought of the mask, an off-white plaster monstrosity with curled holes for the eyes and a smattering of seven horns. I shivered, suddenly cold and in even more desperate need of a drink.

Sandra came close, took my trembling hands in her own, and kissed them.

"When I put it on, I saw hell, souls in agony, and they knew I was watching and they all surged like beggars." I shivered. "That is something no child should see."

Sandra took my drink away and placed it on the counter behind me. She leaned in even closer and kissed my lips. She drew me out of the kitchen, leaving my poor martini to fend for itself. We went to the living room and sat on the couch.

"Tell me the rest of your story," she said.

"The beast was in the mask," I told her. "Once they put it on me, the beast entered my body. The first night I transformed in front of the Great Pyre, it hurt so much that I thought I was dying."

I closed my eyes and saw Juliette standing before me, her arm bandaged, her face as well. When I asked her what happened, she wouldn't say. Finally, my aunt told me that after I transformed, the beast attacked Juliette before it could be restrained.

"I woke seven days later, locked in a room," I told Sandra. "The Sisterhood robbed me of my life. They continue to light the Sacred Fire every seven years. They invoke the beast and I change for seven days. Alone."

Sandra reached over and ran her fingers through my hair.

"Someone very dear to me had been mauled by the beast."

"Who?"

"A girl. Juliette. My first lover. I—the beast scarred her for life."

Sandra gasped. "What happened?"

"When I came back to myself, I ran away to Houston. I was clever enough to tell my father a believable version of the truth. I showed my father the mark. There were several stories circulating at the time about ritual abuse. The story made the news."

"It all sounds very crazy," Sandra said sympathetically.

I touched my chest, absentmindedly covering the star above my breast.

Sandra's hand covered mine.

"The Sisterhood disappeared. Juliette too," I said. "Every seven years, I went back to Salacia to lock myself up, and then I built my own place."

"So what is the beast exactly?" Sandra asked.

I shook my head. "I remember my aunt calling it a familiar."

"Like a witch's familiar?" Sandra asked.

I shrugged. "I suppose it's the Sisterhood's familiar. They draw some kind of power from the Sacred Fire. The beast is part of it."

"And they've never tried to contact you?"

"I would have them all arrested if they did."

Sandra scoffed. "For what, exactly?"

"For making me into a monster," I said, pulling away and moving toward the kitchen. "They stole my childhood. My life."

I reclaimed my martini and took a swig. Sandra entered the kitchen behind me. I didn't turn around and listened to her tidy things.

"I can't begin to try to understand what happened to you, Tinsley," she said. "You don't have to do this alone anymore."

I turned. "I haven't been with anyone since Juliette."

She froze. "You were fourteen—"

"And I ended up hurting her," I said. "So I decided I would never get close enough to hurt anyone again."

"You won't," she insisted.

"You don't know that."

"I'm a little psychic," she said.

"Really?" I asked incredulously.

She left the kitchen and went for her handbag, which she had left by the front door. She returned cradling a colorful scarf in her hands and sat at the kitchen table.

"Fix me one of those martinis."

I brought the ingredients to the table and watched her unwrap a deck of what looked to be tarot cards. She looked up at me with a twinkle in her eye. She motioned for me to sit down.

I watched her stack the cards into a neat deck in between us. They were gilded, and the backs were printed with a textile-like red and white pattern.

"My family has been doing this for generations, the women at least. The story about how it all started is muddled, but my mother taught me, as her mother did and hers before her. It's like our own made-up tarot."

"You don't actually believe you can tell the future with a deck of cards?" I asked.

Sandra smiled smugly. "No, just like I don't believe women can turn into beasts."

"Touché."

"Anyway," she said, "these don't tell the future. They give insight into the present."

"Now that we have that cleared up," I said sarcastically.

Sandra quieted me with a wave of her hand. She split the deck in three piles.

"Now stack those into one, in any order you choose."

I moved to pick up the cards but paused when Sandra spoke.

"Concentrate."

I wiped away my grin and tried to be serious, though I was a little south of tipsy from the alcohol consumption. I picked up the middle stack, placed it on top of the left, and then placed the remaining cards on top.

Sandra raised her eyebrows. She picked up the top half of the deck and put it aside. "I'm going to do what my grandmother called the star draw. It's your present and near future."

She removed cards from the bottom of the deck and arranged them in a circle face down. Sandra flipped the first card over. It showed two fish swimming in opposite directions. I peered down at the stylization, rendered in a vector program.

"Did you design these?"

"From the old ones that belonged to my grandmother," Sandra said. "I wanted to keep it in the same tradition, but a little less crude in the rendering."

"I wondered if you actually had any talent. These are wonderful."

Sandra winked. "Dos Peces, the two fish. Lately, your emotions have been in a state of change, moving in unpredictable tides, in floods. You flow shallow sometimes, narrow in your thinking."

She flipped a second card with a broken heart surrounded by flames.

"Another emotional card. Sorrow has been a part of your life for a long time."

"Duh," I drawled.

"Fine, I'll stop," Sandra said. She reached forward and began to snatch up the draw. "I thought I could share this with you, but I see you're like everyone else…so close-minded."

I covered her hand with my own. The contact startled me, and by the quick draw of her breath, I could tell it startled her too.

"I'm sorry. Please continue."

She looked annoyed but didn't move her hand.

"Please. I'm glad you're here, Sandra, and that I can share this with you."

She withdrew her hand as a slow grin spread across her face. "You're supposed to turn over the third."

I did, saw a feathered quill, and sighed, unimpressed. "That has to be an unemotional card."

"Like you would know," Sandra said. "It means that you observe life and record it all in great detail."

I bent my brow wryly. "How interesting. You rigged these."

"I did not."

"Then it's a card trick."

Sandra turned over a fourth card. "You are ruled by the nature of the fox. You're a loner, and you live in shadow… *mysteriosa*."

"Could the fox be a symbol for the beast?"

"Sure," she said.

Yet there I sat, enrapt, half listening to the words she spoke, more attentive to the lips that spoke them. And her eyes. And the pulse of her neck as she talked. I barely heard a word, the urge to kiss her growing by the second. Maybe it was the gin. Maybe it was the magic in the air.

When she was satisfied with the cards on the table—a bell, a well-dressed lady, and a drunken man—she laughed with finality, noticed me staring, and said I was full of shit. Otherwise, she seemed pleased with the reading.

"What?" she asked.

"You know what," I said.

She chuckled. "Tinsley Swan, you've got that look in your eye. Like you could devour me in one bite."

"Don't joke like that."

She walked behind me. She started in on my shoulders, and I craned my head back to look at her.

"What do you want?" she whispered. "I can go. I can stay. I'd like to stay."

"The beast."

"Tinsley, I didn't see a beast this morning," Sandra said. "Yes, it was scary, not anything I would want to find under my bed, but it didn't look vicious. It looked frightened. Wounded."

I reached out and touched the side of her face. Her eyes were like smoky quartz and smoldered as they searched mine. My fingers disappeared in her hair. I felt her ear, the back of her neck. I pulled her closer, felt her breath as she exhaled, then a vacuum of air as she inhaled, and finally, her lips were on mine.

After a time, she moved away. "I didn't run because I saw you."

She kissed me again; this time there were tears on my face. She wiped them away with her hands. We moved to the couch and kicked off our shoes. She undid a few of my buttons and purposely mussed my hair. She said she liked to see me tousled. I said I liked to see her nude, and flushed at having said such a thing.

We went upstairs. I showed her the bathroom, my bedroom, and then my office.

"You picked the smaller room to sleep in," she said. "You definitely are all business."

She checked out my equipment and ran her fingers over the rolltop. I watched her nervously. One day, I would have to show her the secret room and the postcards. But not tonight. I wanted to forget about the beast and all its trappings.

I took her to my bed. She sat on the edge and removed her shirt and jeans. Her bra and panties were a matching black lace affair. Sandra crawled to the edge of the bed, took my hands, and tried to pull me down with her. I didn't budge, but with a tug of my own, I urged her to her knees and leaned down to kiss her. As we kissed, we sank slowly to the bed, limbs and lips locked.

"You're strong," she whispered. "I felt it last time. Your energy."

"You're drunk," I teased her. I touched between her legs, felt her wetness through the crotch of her panties. "And you're horny."

I slid my pants and underwear off, and she finished with the buttons on my shirt and unclasped my bra. She ran her fingers over the mark above my right breast, a seven-sided star inside a circle in what looked to be reddish brown ink. The sides were elongated and tapered into seven points that extended past the line of the circle.

She bent her head to kiss it, but I stopped her.

"What?"

"I don't want you to touch it," I said. "It feels wrong."

She kissed my lips. "Okay."

Sandra lay on her back. She beckoned me to follow. I covered her body with mine, relished the feel of her skin against mine. She was soft, supple, and fragrant. I nuzzled her belly and breasts, felt her breathing grow ragged. I lowered my head, moved with her until we were pelvis to pelvis, and pushed against her until we were even closer.

Sandra gasped at the contact. We thrust our hips together and back apart. Our legs parted at the thighs and tangled below our knees. I felt her open up to me. We shared a dozen kisses of varying lengths. We whispered curses, and oaths, and pleas that sometimes sounded like our names.

Sometime in the middle of the night, she moved to leave. I reached out for her in the darkness and only caught the warmth she left on the air.

"I don't want to intrude," she whispered sleepily.

"No," I said. "Stay."

Chapter Three

By midweek, the beast had not reared its horned head. With days left until the final change, I tried my best to go about my usual routine. The smells were still a problem throughout the day, but Sandra was always close to soothe me. She came to my office Wednesday morning dressed for business in a pink skirt with matching heels and an ivory-colored blouse that tied at the neck.

She brought me an Earl Grey latte and sat in my spare chair sipping on a frosty coffee with a pile of whipped cream on top.

"Rick Dixon is giving me hell about this stupid stadium contract," she said. "You know he has a major boner for wayfinding graphics."

I made a face at the comment. "Seriously."

She grinned and leaned over. "How are you this morning?"

"Fine and dandy," I said.

"Missed you last night," she whispered.

"I needed to catch up on my sleep," I whispered back. "I put a present in your office."

Her eyes widened. "For real?"

I laughed. "Yeah."

"If this is your way of trying to get rid of me so you can play with your fake livers—"

"I'd be broke by the end of the week."

She laughed. "I know where you live."

That said, she sauntered out of my office to claim her prize, and I actually felt good.

Her perfume lingered. Or maybe it was the beast's sense of smell. I sipped my tea and wondered.

Someone rapped on my door frame, and my father of all people peeked into my office. Our building happened to be one of his properties, but in fifteen years, he had never visited me at work. He filled up the door frame, a tall, lanky man with mahogany skin and gold wire-rim glasses.

"Tinsley." He smiled.

"Dad." I walked around my desk to greet him. "Is everything all right?"

"Fine," he said. "Except my only child never calls me."

"Dad," I drawled as I pulled out a chair for him and perched on the edge of my desk.

"I heard Zidonis was sold," he said. "How are things under the new management?"

"Fine. I've been forced to promotion."

He raised his eyebrows. "That's a big move. It's about time."

"It's a pain," I admitted. "I never get to work from home anymore."

Dad patted my knee with one of his large hands. "Well, I've always admired your work ethic, Tinsley."

I smiled slightly. I knew my father thought my lifestyle odd, but he would never say a word about it. Like me, he lived a solitary life. Most of his social activities were closely related to work. He never remarried or even dated as far as I knew. I could hardly imagine my father being romantically inclined. Our relationship often felt more like one of his business arrangements than anything. Whenever we spent time together, it felt as if he were checking on one of his properties. I suspected that rang true of any other relationships he had.

"I was thinking of visiting Uncle Charles," I said.

He frowned. "That old buzzard?" he asked. "It's time for you to cut ties with those people."

My father despised the Tinsley family, especially after what happened in '83. Even before that fateful summer, he seemed to merely tolerate his in-laws.

"I came to see you about Salacia," he said. "This historical site scene is very big on the island. I was thinking we could offer it for sale as a private or public property."

"You want to sell Salacia?" I asked.

Dad sighed. "Let that place go. After what happened I'm surprised you've held on to it for so long."

"I don't need the money," I said.

He chuckled. "You do plan on getting old and retiring someday, don't you?"

"Do you?" I asked.

He laughed. "I do and I assure you, I plan to go big."

"Of course you do, Dad," I said. I thought about Salacia and the cost to keep up the place each year. There really was no reason to keep the house. After my mother's death and my aunt Quinn's disappearance, I inherited what was left of the Tinsley holdings after decades of fiscal irresponsibility.

"I'll think about it," I said.

Another knock at the door. Sandra entered flashing her million-dollar smile.

"Tinsley, I didn't know you had a visitor."

Yeah, right. I surmised with dread that I would have to introduce them.

"Sandra. This is my father, Stephen Swan. Dad, this is Sandra Ortega, the new management here."

My father stood and shook her hand. "It's nice to meet you."

"You as well," Sandra said wryly.

"I came by to discuss some family business with Tinsley," he said. "It seems we've reached the part of our negotiations where I back away and give her time to think."

Sandra beamed. "You know Tinsley; she doesn't jump headfirst into anything."

My father agreed and placed his arm around me in a side hug. "Let's go to dinner soon."

We said our good-byes and he left.

Sandra let out a squeal. "Wow. I see where you get your stiffness."

"Ha," I said.

"I had to come by and be nosy." She grinned. "And to thank you for my pin."

"I'm glad you like it."

She leaned closer to whisper. "I'll thank you properly tonight."

With a wink, she left me standing there in my office alone.

"How am I supposed to get any work done?" I asked the empty office.

My next move was to somehow salvage what remained of the day. I checked email and the headlines at the *Democracy Now* website, until finally, I was able to settle down enough to get started on my main task for the day—making an animated diagram of a heart dissection. I uploaded the file of a previous heart and began to make an exact copy in separate three-dimensional parts.

Before I knew it, two o'clock had come, long past the lunch hour. I nibbled at some avocado salad from the previous night's dinner while I worked.

My cell rang. I recognized the number on the readout as Jimmy, brother of Cosmo and regular provider of postcards for my collection for the past twelve years. I let it ring until the voice mail picked up the call. Jimmy dutifully left a message.

I listened to it immediately.

Jimmy's voice echoed through a haze of static. "Hey, Tinsley, I know you're probably busy at work. I've got a beautiful girl in my clutches, or let's just say I have access to her. Come by this evening and we'll discuss her."

I grinned and hoped this was not a farce. Another girl? Jimmy was very curious about what Cosmo had sold me. I reckoned he had been holding out on me in hopes of one-upping his brother.

At five o'clock, I walked down to Sandra's office to arrange dinner plans.

"You're taking me for Italian," she said. "Out. Away from the Batcave."

She said she would text me in two hours and that the place was not too far from my house. It gave me plenty of time to go see Jimmy.

I drove to the Heights, a large suburb just beyond Midtown. Jimmy's shop squatted on an otherwise empty lot at a busy intersection. He came limping out of the back as I entered. There was no quaint bell, and everything was strewn about. Crushed and torn boxes overflowed with VHS cassettes, records, reels of film, comic books, and sports memorabilia. Jimmy dealt in what he called collectibles. There was not a piece of china, crystal, or cameo to be found in his shop. There was a shelf full of action figures both in and out of the box, and another of a mixture of books from trade back to leather-bound. A few dusty red leather chairs flanked a coffee table with *Playboy* magazines from the seventies fanned out beneath a ray gun prop from some science fiction film.

"Tinsley." He beamed.

I had never asked about his condition, but guessed it to be a severe scoliosis. The affliction seemed to affect his spine and caused it to be severely curved. One of his hips tilted higher than the other, causing a hitch in his gait. His shoulders were hunched and askew in the same angle as his pelvis. Otherwise, he was surprisingly handsome with frosty blond hair and pale lashes over his green eyes. His good looks compounded his physical defects.

"You survived my brother, I see." He limped backward.

"He was nice enough."

He seemed to think we shared a deeper camaraderie than we actually did, and always tried to insinuate himself further into my life. I tolerated this less than good-naturedly, and it probably came off as bitchy.

"Did Cosmo make you participate in one of his tea ceremonies?"

I nodded.

"What a queer. No offense there, Tinsley."

"None taken," I said bitterly. "What have you got for me?"

"A beauty," he answered, and removed a glossy photo from beneath a stack of paperwork, then slid it across the counter.

I glanced down at the photo, which turned out to be a flyer.

"What is this?"

He grinned. "Take a good look at it."

I saw familiar heavy-lidded eyes and curves beneath a pink corset with black laces, but the picture was modern, in color, with a soft gauzy photo-editing filter. Garish pink, glitter-script type read *Girls. Live Shows @ Little Foxes*.

In smaller print was an address of a street I knew vaguely.

"Is this Photoshopped or something?"

"She's hot, isn't she?"

"This is one of the girls I have already."

He laughed and leaned on the counter. "You've been looking at those black-and-whites too long, Tinsley. Time for you to see some real live Technicolor girls."

"Have you seen her?" I pointed to the picture. "With your own eyes?"

"Yeah, that's Leda," he said, his voice taking a sly tone. "I saw her just last week."

"Impossible."

Jimmy shook his head. "Go check her out for yourself. This is a special guest invitation I was given to hand to someone discreet. They are very selective when choosing their clientele."

I barely heard him. My horned Golden Goddess, this so-called Leda, lay on her stomach dressed in a corset, stockings, and garters with bows, on a pile of cushions surrounded by black. She looked directly into the camera, a slight smile on her parted lips.

"This is so strange. Cosmo—"

"What did he have for you anyway?" Jimmy asked. "Nothing as good as the stuff I get."

I inspected the flyer closely in the dim light of the shop. Perhaps Jimmy was right and I had been staring at those old postcards for so long I was beginning to see the girls everywhere.

"She's a fucking model too," he said and whistled. "She's the face of this new tequila coming out in July—Bacchanista."

I looked up at Jimmy. He nodded suggestively.

"Is this place…legal?"

He shrugged his misshapen shoulders. "It's not like anyone is tossing money at dancing girls. In fact it's very classy, very discreet, definitely—like I said—your type of place."

I rolled my eyes.

"Just go in and tell them Jimmy sent you, but don't expect the royal treatment right off," he explained. "You can see Leda or any other girl they have for a private show, and things can get more intimate if you've got the cash."

I made a face of disgust. What I disliked most about Jimmy, besides his outright crudeness, was his assumption that I was some aging yuppie with a secret fetish, like he had something on me.

I glanced back down at the flyer. "It doesn't seem the sort of place I'd be interested in, Jimmy. It looks shady."

He seemed a little upset by the remark. "I thought you were a big wheel, Tinsley."

"What do you mean?"

"You know, a professional broad who knows what she wants and goes for it."

I almost laughed in his face. "I'm a bit more complicated than that, Jimmy."

"So it's a maybe?" he asked and reached out. "Then give it back and I can hand it off to someone else who can appreciate it."

I held on to the card. "Well, can't you get another?"

The corners of his lips pulled down and he groaned. "No. Like I said, Little Foxes is not the kind of place that lets just anyone off the street in."

"I'll give you fifty bucks for it. I may decide to go."

He stared at me for a moment and grinned. "So you were shitting me about not going."

"Perhaps."

He nodded in appreciation. "I get it, Tinsley. You like to play it close."

I dug out my wallet, but he waved me off. "Keep the flyer. Just don't forget to tell that dickhead Claudio that it was me who sent you."

"Thanks, Jimmy. I owe you one."

Once home, I hurried to my study and the rolltop desk. I pulled out the box, found the two postcards of my goddess, and laid them on either side of the flyer. I studied the three photos side by side, black-and-white, and sepia tone, and full gloss color, until no doubt remained of the resemblance.

I sat back in my seat. Of ancient lady cults, beasts, and Mexican gypsies, this was the one thing I just could not fathom. As if on cue, Sandra called to tell me she had texted directions to the restaurant and that she was leaving her house.

I left right away. Sandra's directions led me to a red-brick building around the corner from a small park presided over by a large oak. She waited for me at a corner table with a bottle of wine. My heart lifted at the sight of her, waiting for me, and smiling once she spotted me.

She wore a soft, pink T-shirt with some designer logo over her breast. The collar dipped into a deep V that revealed a nice view of her cleavage. She smiled at me when I sat.

"You look cute."

"I bothered to go home and change," she said tartly.

"Didn't know that was a prerequisite."

She grinned and poured me a glass of wine and we toasted.

"How is everything with…you know?" she asked. "How do you feel?"

"I feel great, now."

She sighed and rested her chin on her hand. She looked beautiful, and I felt compelled to append my previous comment on her cuteness.

I glanced at my menu. "I've been very hungry lately. That usually happens around this time."

"Oh?" Sandra put down her wineglass. "Is that a heads-up?"

"Yes."

"I wonder how that works," she said. "Like is it totally metaphysical, or are there some traces of it, like in your blood or your bones?"

I shrugged. "I try to avoid the doctor. And I've never gotten sick since the initiation." A waiter came and took our orders. Sandra insisted that we split a plate of veal parmigiana so we could have room for an appetizer and dessert. We had fritto misto, a mix of meats and calamari deep-fried in batter, and after our entrée, panna cotta, which reminded me of the Mexican flan, drenched in black raspberry liqueur.

I hardly ever ate out. I saw it as more of a social thing and always felt weird when I found myself in a restaurant alone.

Sandra was of course in her element. We went through a bottle and a half of wine by the end of dessert and chatted until the staff began to stack the chairs.

We paid and walked out, where we found the night hot yet breezy. The clouds moved fast above us, and I knew there would be rain before morning. Sandra leaned on me and giggled on our way to the parking lot.

I directed us to the little park and we walked along the semi-lit path. She stopped as we passed beneath. "What?" I asked.

She grinned and her eyes glinted, even in such low light. "There is something about you, Tinsley Swan. And I'm not just being desperate and horny right now."

"Don't forget drunk," I added.

We laughed. We kissed. She tasted of raspberry liqueur.

Behind us, someone cleared her throat. Sandra stepped away from me, but held on to my hand. I muttered an apology to the person offended by our lesbian PDA.

"Hello, Sister of Flame," the stranger said with a French-tinged accent. I tilted my head. No one had referred to me by that title since the summer of '83.

"Juliette?"

She stepped from the shadows, as lithe at ever, and still heartbreakingly lovely. She reached out for me and I pulled her into a limp hug. When we pulled away, I could feel Sandra's eyes on us like daggers.

I turned to her. "This is Juliette."

"The Juliette? The Sisterhood Juliette?"

I nodded. Juliette hissed. "What have you told her?" she asked.

"Everything," I said. "It's public knowledge, you know. The press had a field day. Everyone was up in arms about satanic cults—"

"An old wound that the Sisterhood has nearly recovered

from," Juliette said. "We need your help, Tinsley. The goddess walks."

I took Sandra's hand and walked away from the woman I had not seen in over twenty years.

"We've always watched over you," she called behind us.

"Sure," I said without turning. "Quinn continues to burn the great pyre every seven years, and turn me into a beast."

"Quinn is dead, Tinsley."

I stepped back, not sure how I should take the news. The woman who had cursed me was dead. Sandra moved next to me in the semi-darkness and took my hand.

"I lead the Sisterhood now," Juliette said.

"You've been lighting the fire?" I asked.

"I have to, Tinsley," she said. "There is so much you missed out on learning."

"Trust me, I've gotten all the education I need."

"The goddess walks." Juliette said that strange phrase again. "The beast seeks her. That is what's different about this cycle and why I'm here asking for your help."

I stopped and she stepped around me, next to Sandra. I could see her face better, and the scars left by the beast's attack, slanted welts across her cheek, above and below her eye, a different texture than the smooth ebony of her skin. She wore black jeans, boots, and a black T-shirt.

"You may have forgotten us, but we have struggled on," she said with conviction. "The Sisterhood never fully disbanded. We went underground, and believe what you will, but we watched over you."

I shook my head. "I'm sorry my aunt stole your life like she stole mine."

She reached out and touched my arm. "I stayed willingly, at least to learn more about the Sisterhood, and why the things they did were necessary."

"Why?" I asked. "There is no reason you can come up with where I can forgive this curse." I put my hand on my chest, on the mark of the seven-sided star beneath my shirt.

Juliette looked to Sandra, who watched silently, expectantly.

"I don't want to explain in front of her," Juliette said.

"Who am I going to tell?" Sandra asked. "Who would believe me?"

Juliette didn't reply. "It's just strange that you've been alone so long, and this woman…"

Sandra straightened. "This woman?" I said.

"That she should enter your life at this moment, and you tell her everything. Has she seen the beast?"

"Yes," I said. "She was there when I transformed."

"When the goddess walks, the beast will seek her out."

I chortled. "You think Sandra is a goddess."

Sandra gave my arm a push. "Why is that so hard to believe?"

I looked to Juliette, who reached behind her back and pulled a metal box from a knapsack. I recognized it immediately.

"The embers from the last pyre," I said and glanced at Sandra out of the corner of my eyes.

"No way," she said in disbelief.

Juliette opened the box, the glow of the bits of burning timber illuminating her face. She reached in, scooped out some embers, and flung them out at Sandra.

Sandra stepped back, but it was too late. The embers broke into pieces at her feet, bounced off the pink slingbacks beneath the cuffs of her jeans, and fell in little explosions of sparks on the gravel. She looked up as she kicked at the little fiery pieces.

"Goddamnit, these are Zanotti."

"What was that all about?" I asked Juliette.

"The embers would have harmed the goddess," she said solemnly. "I'm sorry."

"So explain," Sandra insisted.

Juliette sighed. "Every seven years the stars here in the physical realm and those of the underworld line up identically. The wall between the worlds weakens and so we light the Sacred Fire to strengthen it."

"And I turn into the beast."

Juliette shook her head. "The beast is drawn to the fire, like all creatures of the underworld. Every seventy years, the Lost Goddess walks the earth and must be burned in the Sacred Fire. The beast is her familiar, and she needs to claim it so she can return to the underworld."

I exchanged a puzzled glance with Sandra, and then asked Juliette, "What does that have to do with anything?"

Juliette looked to Sandra. "The Lost Goddess. You know her as the red woman who rides the red beast of the apocalypse. *La Gran Ramera de Babilonia.*"

"The what?" I asked.

Sandra stepped away; that sparkle I enjoyed earlier was gone. "The Whore of Babylon," she said.

I frowned, vaguely familiar with the allegory from the Book of Revelations. "Really? Isn't that a bit patriarchal for your all-female cult? I thought the trend was to turn all the whores of the Bible into heroines."

"Tinsley," Sandra gasped. "She's talking about the end of the world."

"She's full of shit," I said. "The Sisterhood is just a bunch of depraved old biddies with a little bit of knowledge and power who like to ruin the lives of young girls."

I claimed Sandra's hand and marched away from Juliette and her lies.

"You're the last of Alexandrine's line," she called.

"Then let the curse die with me," I said over my shoulder.

I stalked to my car and climbed in. My heart stopped when

Sandra didn't join me. She peered at me through the driver's side window, her eyes haunted. At last, the curse had driven her away, just as I predicted.

"I drove here, remember?" Sandra said.

"Come home with me," I said, prepared to beg.

She nodded. "Lead the way."

She trailed me in her car, and once she parked inside my gate, she followed me silently into the house. I offered her a drink, but she refused and told me that I shouldn't. I ignored her and went for the bottle of Old Raj.

"You don't actually believe that nonsense Juliette was spouting?"

Sandra came into the kitchen and took my arms at the wrist and gently pulled me to the couch. She hugged me around the waist.

"It frightened you," I said.

"Yes," Sandra said. "You should have heard her out."

"Really?"

"She sounded really desperate and scared," Sandra said. "She seems worried over what this Lost Goddess can do."

"She's brainwashed," I said. "A fanatic."

"Why would she come to you after all these years unless something was up?"

"I don't care what she's got going on," I said.

"She was talking apocalypse," Sandra said gravely. "The end of the world."

"Bullshit." I paced around the couch. "How dare they? Aunt Quinn disappeared before she could answer for her crimes, and my mother killed herself that winter. They're both dead and gone."

Sandra peered up at me. "You didn't tell me that, Tinsley."

"They all chose the Sisterhood and left me alone with the beast," I said. "Even Juliette. You know, for years, I fantasized that she would show up and we would be together."

Sandra put her arms around me and rested her head on my chest. "I'm sorry that you had to be alone for so long."

I held her close. "It doesn't matter. The beast is my responsibility. It'll die with me, and in the meantime I'll just have to live my life in seven-year increments."

"You don't know that," Sandra said against my breast. "You hardly know anything about the Sisterhood."

I backed away from her a bit. "Which side are you on?"

"She just looked so haunted," Sandra said.

I dropped my arms. "And me?"

"You should have heard her out," she said.

"They fooled me once. I won't allow them to drag me into their shit again." I returned to the couch and sat down. "Are you frightened of me now?"

"No," Sandra said. "Never."

She brought her body close to mine until she was practically sitting in my lap, her legs wrapped around me as we kissed. Her arms enveloped me as well. I buried my face in her neck and ran my tongue over the flesh there. She shivered all around me. I lost myself for a moment in her kiss and embrace. The pull of her limbs constricted and loosened.

Her lips found my ear. "Take me upstairs," she whispered.

Out of habit, I felt a twinge of anxiety at having another person in my home and so close to my secrets. This was Sandra, though. She was safe. She wasn't afraid. The embers had ruined her designer shoes, but she hadn't gone up in flames.

I took her hand, and for the rest of the night, did everything she asked of me and more.

❖

I woke sometime during the night. A voice from an unknown dream. Sandra snored softly next to me. I reached under the covers and stroked her hip. She muttered in her sleep but didn't stir. I slid out of my bed and padded down the hall clad only in my underwear.

I went to my office and opened the rolltop. In the cover of darkness, I removed the box of postcards and found my Golden Goddess and the flyer by touch. I lay them side by side on the big metal desk and turned on the light.

They certainly looked to be the same girl.

I had discovered many things that summer in '83. The armored woman was the only thing I willingly absconded with that eighth night, a full day after I changed back into myself.

The Golden Goddess. Why had I chosen that name?

"I was a fourteen-year-old kid, that's why," I said. "With a penchant for mythology."

I remembered Juliette's words from earlier: "The goddess walks. The beast seeks her."

Alone in my office, I answered her. "There's only one way to find out."

I packed the original pictures into a Mylar pouch and slipped them into my briefcase. I then returned to bed and snuggled next to Sandra in spooning position. I smiled a bit to myself. I had never imagined myself as a snuggler. This time, she did stir. She turned around in my arms and began to kiss me.

She giggle-mumbled something unintelligible in a sexy, sleep voice.

"What?" I whispered.

Sandra snaked an arm around my neck, placed her hand at the base of my skull, and pulled herself closer until we were pelvis to pelvis.

"Are you even awake?" I asked.

She relaxed against me and rested her head on my pillow. In a matter of seconds, I could hear her light snores.

I smiled. "Good night."

Chapter Four

I had never been to the Shady Oaks Assisted Living complex before. The place looked generic enough. The lawns around the place were well kept. Several residents wandered the smooth cement paths with their various walking aids, enjoying the day before the sun rose too high.

A security guard allowed me past the main gate, and I parked in the visitor's lot. I felt nervous to be visiting Uncle Charles. I had only met the man several times during my life, the last being my mother's funeral. I controlled the trust that provided for his stay at Shady Oaks, just as other Tinsley women had controlled other stages of his life. An attendant led me to Uncle Charles, who was playing chess in the game room with another attendant.

He glanced up at me, and his peanut butter skin actually blanched. His white brow furrowed, and he used his rook to put his opponent in check. The attendant let out a short, disappointed groan.

"Take your time," Uncle Charles said. "It seems I have a visitor."

The man turned from the chessboard to give me a distracted once-over. "Your daughter?"

"My grand-niece."

"Hello," I said. "How have you been, Uncle Charles?"

"Fine. Fine," he said. "Though I'm not sure now."

"I wanted to ask a question about something I found at Salacia," I said.

He gave a dry chuckle and stared at me with cold, rheumy eyes. "I doubt there's anything I can tell you about Salacia that you don't already know."

I straightened and looked around the room. At least we were on the same page. I wondered if he was angry with me about the disappearance of his niece, and the death of another. I had always assumed he felt no ties to the family, being a male.

"Well, there are some pictures I found in the library, and as I understand, that was once your domain."

Uncle Charles didn't seem to hear me. He had returned to studying his chessboard as his opponent made another move. He clucked his tongue and muttered something under his breath.

"Pictures," he said. "Pictures."

"Yes," I said. "Perhaps you can help me identify the person in them."

He looked up at me again. "Of course. Tinsley. That name," he said in a musing tone, as if he were just realizing who exactly I was. "They were very excited when you were born. You would have thought Quinn was having the baby herself."

He chuckled again. It sounded like a dusty, rarely used thing. "There was a big party, the last one that involved everyone, not one of those where only the women were invited. We all posed for a picture together. Your father didn't come along. A wise man indeed."

I cleared my throat and glanced at the attendant, who turned around to look at me with a bit more interest. I looked back to Uncle Charles, who narrowed his eyes bitterly. The light from the window suffused his white hair with a sunny glow, and he looked like Moses returning from the mountain.

"Let's see your pictures," he grumbled. "So Miss Tinsley can return to her life, and I can finish out my days here."

He waved the attendant away, and I sat in his place. I removed the pictures of Leda from my satchel and passed him the one of her dressed in armor. He caught it between trembling fingers, a slight grin on his face.

"Letty," he said simply.

"That's her name?"

"Yes," he said, longing in his voice. "I met her through my older brother, Malcolm, when I ran away to New Orleans."

"So she was there?"

He nodded. "Your great-grandmother was very displeased with Malcolm. He rebelled against the matriarchy, you could say, and he hated those others that would come every seven years and look down their noses at him as we were shipped off to camp."

I raised my eyebrows. "You wanted to be a rebel too."

He smiled. "It was 1939, a dangerous time for a soft, colored boy to travel through the South alone. I made it, and Malcolm was there in New Orleans taking pictures of naked girls."

"And Leda—Letty was one of those girls?"

"Everyone loved Letty," Uncle Charles said. "She was like a ray of sunshine wherever she went, and Malcolm spent his last dime on her. We had to go crawling back to Salacia with our tails between our legs." He turned the picture over and his grin sagged to a more grave expression. "We took Letty."

A short gasp escaped my lips.

"Then you know what happened to her?" Uncle Charles said hopefully.

I shook my head. "What do you know?"

"Malcolm and I thought that if we went to Salacia just before one of those seven-year meetings, we could get some money from Mother and leave," he said, his clouded eyes glazed over as he looked back into the past. "Mother welcomed us. She and our sister, your grandmother Cornelia, welcomed Letty and offered her a room. Malcolm didn't want to cause a row, and he didn't go to Letty's room when the house was quiet. We got drunk in the library."

Uncle Charles's voice choked on emotion, and he reached into his pocket for a handkerchief. "The next morning, Letty was gone," Charles said. "We looked all over for her, but could find no trace, but Malcolm knew. Cornelia had scratches on her arms, and there was a scorch mark in the room where Letty had slept, like a fire had burned."

"Did you call the authorities?" I asked.

He laughed. "We didn't dare. We were frightened of Mother and Cornelia's cult. We knew they burned a big fire out on the lawn every seven years. Malcolm and I left and did not return for a long time."

"And Letty?" I asked. "Do you know where she came from?"

"She never talked of her past," he said. "She was a creature of pure delight: dancing, drinking, playing, fucking…she made a man feel like a million bucks." He placed a worn and wrinkled hand over the picture. "May I keep this?"

I felt something protective rise up inside me, almost like the beast would. "I could mail you a copy," I told him.

He frowned. "What would you want with it?" he asked. "Why would you come here asking about her? You didn't come here for nothing."

"I was only curious," I said.

I reached over the chessboard to retrieve the picture, and Uncle Charles grabbed my wrist in a viselike grip. I tried to escape his grip and knocked over all his chess pieces.

"Selfish woman," he growled. "Too stupid to let Mother's cult go about their business to see something greater than yourself."

"They frightened you and Malcolm," I said. "You said so yourself. They did something with Letty and you did nothing."

He let go of me and I stood, snatching the picture. He bowed his head and covered his face with his hands. The attendant returned, a look of concern on his face as he went to Uncle Charles. "What's going on here?" he asked.

"I'm sorry," I said. "We were only talking. I may have mentioned a family issue that upset him."

"He gets like this sometimes," the attendant told me. "Maybe if he got more visitors…"

I found myself apologizing again. "My family was never very close."

"Everybody has an excuse," the young man mumbled and turned away to console Uncle Charles. He shrank before my eyes, his elbows on his knees, his head down as he began to sob. I stared, not sure what to do or say. I backed away a few steps, ready to flee. Charles glanced up at me as he dispassionately wiped the tears off his cheeks and struggled to compose himself.

"If I had known you would get upset, I wouldn't have come," I said.

He snarled. "You Tinsley women are all alike," he said. "So high and mighty, with your secrets. We should all be glad to live in your shadow."

"There are no more secrets," I said.

"There are plenty," he said, his face dry, his breathing less unsteady. "Now don't leave here and forget what you promised to send me."

"I won't," I told him.

❖

That evening, I sat in my parked car. Despite the cool air that rolled through the vents, I felt as if the sinking sun slowly roasted my skin. Once again, I was in one of those nearly forgotten corners of town with the hopes of catching a glimpse of the woman called Leda. After visiting Uncle Charles, I went to work and scanned the picture of the woman he called Letty. I printed a copy and had it sent to him by courier. I found that I couldn't concentrate at all on work. I kept sliding the pictures out of my satchel and looking at them. I made dinner plans with Sandra for six and went to the address on the flyer Jimmy had given me.

Little Foxes was housed in an old tan brick building that squatted in a questionable neighborhood. My hopes were to happen to see her without having to actually go inside.

There were several businesses on the block: a pawnshop, a liquor store, a barbeque joint, and a tire shop. All the parking was on the street, so I parked and sat inconspicuously with a view of the entrance. In the two and a half hours I waited, two men left and a woman entered. They looked like normal people, in normal clothes. I had done my research. Little Foxes was not listed among the city's businesses, most likely because places called modeling studios were often raided by the police under suspicions of illicit practices, as they were fronts for prostitution.

Discouraged and out of time, I went to Sandra's for the evening. She accused me of being distant and as aloof as the day we were introduced. She forced me to sit with her and look through a picture album of her childhood on the Texas-Mexico border. I got into her record collection and we slow danced to Al Green until things got serious. I stayed the night.

I returned to Little Foxes the next afternoon with several bottles of iced tea, some light snacks, and a pair of opera glasses inherited from my mother. I waited three hours before gathering enough courage to take a stroll past the building. I paused on the sidewalk just feet from the entrance. Up close, I noticed that the cracked brick crawling with a tiny green vine budding with purple flowers was merely an old façade from the twenties. A stone placard over the lintel of the entrance read Fox, and I wondered if that was how Little Foxes got its name.

I then noticed a man who seemed completely composed of rolls of fat trundling toward me on a motorized wheelchair. He grinned and poured new sweat that mixed with the yellowed stains of old on his white T-shirt.

"Hey, sister," he hollered. "You got any change?"

I backed up a few steps, turned, fled to my car, and drove away from that place. I spotted a side alley as I made my escape. I made a mental note to inspect it the next day, but I never made it.

CHAPTER FIVE

The next day was Friday. That morning, I woke with the Little Foxes stalking game on my mind, and I decided that the coast was clear to stay at home. I planned to work through the morning and spend the entire afternoon in my car watching for Leda. Work ran over, though, and I finished with my last project a little after noon.

When I went out to my car, those Sun Monster kids were out playing. They gathered at the gate and called me Professor Swiggleslock. I smiled at their game, only because I had my own to play that afternoon. The character card one of them had handed me still lay in one of the cup holders between the Volvo's front seats.

As I cruised out onto the street, my phone rang. I answered it as I carefully negotiated the crowd of small children playing in the street.

"Hello, Sister of Flame."

I rolled my eyes. "How did you get this number, Juliette?"

"We need to talk," she said. "I know you've discovered the Lost Goddess's incarnation."

I turned off my street, not sure what to say.

"I have no idea what you're talking about," I said.

"The place called Little Foxes," Juliette said. "What would

Sandra say if she knew you were hanging around such an establishment?"

A hot flash of anger passed through my body. "It's none of her business, or yours, since we're on the topic."

I ended the call, fuming. My phone chirped as another call came through. I checked the readout. Juliette again. The bitch just didn't know when to quit. I answered just to tell her off.

"This is harassment, you know," I said.

"Tinsley, why did you go visit Charles?"

I drove to a line of cars waiting at a congested stoplight. I looked in my rearview mirror expecting to see her following me.

"Are you even in the country legally?" I asked distractedly.

"You need to put your bitterness aside," Juliette said. "If the beast and the Lost Goddess were ever to come together—"

"Not my problem," I said and ended the call.

The traffic in the other lane coasted forward. A taxi van rolled past me and stopped. A placard mounted on the trunk advertised a new premium tequila. A familiar face stared out at me from the photo below overly gilded script.

My Golden Goddess, also known as Leda, dressed just as she was in the flyer Jimmy had given me. In this shot, she leaned forward showing her small but shapely cleavage, her hands cradling what looked to be a wine bottle. Her expression was sleepy and sultry. My phone chirped.

Behind me, some idiot honked. Traffic was moving. Before I could tear my eyes away from the billboard, I pressed the gas a little too enthusiastically. The car in front of me had barely moved a foot. I stomped on my brakes to avoid a collision. Tires screamed in protest. A loud bang followed, and then I heard the roar of glass shattering as my back window exploded into bits. For an instant, the violent impact jarred my world. The force threw me forward. The seat belt jerked me back into an upright position.

Beneath the blur of tears that sprang into my eyes, I saw the men on the street and the asshole behind me rocking behind the wheel as his car shook from the collision. Then things were quiet, except for a ringing in my ears. I reached out numbly, unlatched the door, and climbed out of the Volvo on unsteady legs.

The douche bag who rear-ended me shouted in a high-pitched voice as he grabbed the back of his neck. I couldn't understand his words, but I could understand his anger. I felt it radiating at me like heat. This aroused and strengthened the beast.

My right shoe tightened around my foot, suddenly three sizes too small. I knew through my numbness that the hair had grown back on the top of my foot. My hand began to chime and buzz. The phone still remained clutched tightly in my fist. I turned it over in my hand, and for a few seconds, it was a foreign object that I regarded as an insect in a shiny black and silver carapace. I knew then that I saw the world through the eyes of the beast.

Someone touched my shoulder gently. I nearly jumped out of my skin. A man in a hard hat inspected me with dark, darting eyes, a look of concern on his face.

"Are you all right, lady?"

I tried to speak, but no words would come. I looked at the back of my car. The glass of the hatchback had shattered, the section where the taillight had been left hollow, and red plastic shards littered the pavement like confetti.

The owner of the car I rear-ended sat on the curb. He pointed at me and swore as a suited man attended him. I looked for the taxi van. The billboard of my Golden Goddess blocked out the sun. In my hand, the phone continued to buzz. Once again, I knew its purpose. The beast was fading back. My humanity flooded back into my body. I willed myself to answer.

"Hello?" I burbled.

"If you won't listen to me, listen to Sandra."

My fingers opened. The phone fell from my hands and clattered to the street. Someone asked if I wanted to go to the hospital. The sturdy hands of men guided me. In the distance, an ambulance wailed.

❖

"I'm fine," I said. The EMT removed the blood pressure cuff from my arm. She didn't look old enough to buy cigarettes, let alone administer medical treatment. I sat in the back of the ambulance listening to this kid lecture me about my vitals. I saw Sandra pull up to the scene. She stepped out of her car, her face strained with concerned.

"What happened?"

"Someone rear-ended me."

"Are you…ill?"

"No," I said, directing my gaze to the EMT. "I'm fine. Now."

"Then it's settled," Sandra said.

She assured the young medic that she would take care of me, and we walked to my car to survey the damage. The back of the Volvo was ruined. Sandra helped me gather my personal effects, including the Professor Swiggleslock card.

"And you make fun of my card tricks." She grinned.

I shrugged as I signed for a random tow truck dispatched by my insurance company and then watched the man haul it off.

"That asshole hit you pretty hard," Sandra said as we climbed into her SUV.

"Well, I was distracted," I said. "Juliette called to hassle me about her Lost Goddess."

"How'd she get your number?"

"I don't know," I grumbled. I sank down in my seat and let my thoughts wander to the ad on the taxicab, to Leda.

Sandra took me home and waited on me hand and foot before she left again to tie up some loose ends at work. I tried to work on a project, but my thoughts kept wandering to Leda. There wasn't much I could do with no wheels. I retrieved the two photos of my Golden Goddess and their modern counterpart. I Googled Bacchanista Tequila and clicked on the first link.

A short animated Flash intro played through, and the website's home page appeared wreathed in some antique, bronze-colored filigree popular with designers. The site was slick to say the least. There was a still of her in a shiny black leather corset trimmed in what looked to be barbed wire, a blackened monocle over one eye, and metallic razor tips at the ends of her fingernails. She held a bottle in one hand, a shot glass in the other, over-pouring as rivulets ran over the glass. Her eyes were a violet color. More photo-editing magic?

Fortune turned in my favor when the insurance company delivered a car to my front door. All I had to do was sign for it. After the insurance agent left, I hung out at the gate looking for any sign of Juliette. I saw those Sun Monster kids across the street playing. The boy who had given me the Professor Swiggleslock card came over.

"Hey," I said. "Have you seen a strange lady around here with scars on her face?"

He grinned and nodded solemnly. "She talks funny."

"Are you shitting me?" I said more to myself than the kid.

"She's a Dark Agent," he volunteered. He brought out his deck and shuffled it. He showed me a picture of a woman in a black trench coat with silver buttons and a hat with a large brim that shaded her face.

"Does she pass by my house?" I asked.

"She waits at the corner." He pointed toward the end of the street. "In a black car. She ain't there today."

"Good," I said. I reached into my wallet and gave him a ten-dollar bill.

He smiled, revealing two missing bottom teeth. "You want me to tell you when she's there?"

I paused to think how that would help me. There weren't many ways out, as Valentine was a one-way street. I looked through the bars of my gate at the kid who stared up at me expectantly.

"What's your name?"

"Bobby," he said, folding and unfolding his prize.

"Okay, Bobby," I said. "You tell me when she's here."

He nodded and sprinted away.

I climbed into the rental and drove to Little Foxes.

Chapter Six

A s the sun began to sink low, I cruised past Little Foxes in the rental car several times before parking. For fifteen minutes, I sat out front and stared at the place and tried to plan what would happen once I walked inside. This was more than a reconnaissance mission; this would be direct contact. I only needed a glimpse of her and I would know.

When the street was empty of cars and pedestrians, I made my move.

At the entrance, I paused to steel myself. I smelled something small and dead in the sparse shrubbery, perhaps a bird or a rat. The purple flowers on the vines gave a sweet, green odor. A feverish flash ran through my body, and I knew the beast was near.

"No, not now."

I waited, measuring the weight of the beast's presence as if it were the beginning of a toothache. The beast stayed low, so I straightened my shoulders and entered Little Foxes.

The place was still laid out like a house. In the dim foyer, I made out the shape of a podium of dark wood. A velvet rope blocked the way behind it. I tried to peer past, but not a glint of light from outside crept beyond the rope.

I cleared my throat and gave a timid hello.

No answer. I debated leaving.

"Who the fuck is it?" a voice bellowed, startling me.

The outline of a large man filled the hall beyond. A light winked on overhead and I saw him—beefy with hairy forearms and a bald head and a short beard. He wore a white tank top, yellowed from sweat around the neck. He also wore several thick gold chains with various medallions. The largest had the name Claudio shaped into it. He had a large keg belly and flabby pectorals like misshapen breasts.

"Jimmy sent me," I stammered.

Claudio frowned. He had heavy jowls, and his words growled from them cloaked in a dark Eastern European accent.

"The goat man." He came close to inspect me with tiny dark eyes. "What do you want?"

I dug into my satchel and removed the glossy flyer.

"Okay, you wanna see a girl," Claudio stated impatiently.

I pointed my finger at Leda's image. "This girl."

He laughed. "The fucking lezbos are coming out of the woodwork for Leda."

"Pardon?"

"That's what you are, eh? A lezbo?"

"I don't think that is any of your business."

Claudio laughed cruelly. "It is my business. You are here to see my girls. So you're either a lezbo or a cop."

I felt my face burn with anger and embarrassment.

"What sort of establishment is this? I didn't come here to be mistreated."

"You came here." He pointed to the ceiling. "You're a stranger to me and you want me to kiss your ass. Jimmy should have explained."

I paused, stared at him, and remembered Jimmy's warning. He hadn't just been giving me a hard time. This was his domain, snarky and sleazy, not mine.

I turned to leave.

"Wait," he shouted. "Are you leaving? Without seeing Leda?"

Claudio had already noticed my urgency and adroitly played it against me. I turned back and glanced down at the flyer.

"How much?"

He gave a mock shrug as if he were not sure. He then turned down the corners of his stubble-covered lips. "You want an unscheduled private show? That'll be three hundred."

"Dollars?" I balked at the price. "Highway robbery."

"Look, lady, you want to come back for a scheduled show?" he asked. "It's only one fifty."

I imagined being faced with strangers, all of them looking at Leda, and I shook my head. I'd had the foresight to go to the ATM and withdrawn as much as the machine would allow in one transaction.

I reached into my satchel again, this time to remove my wallet and count out the bills Claudio demanded. He took them between two fingers as stubby and fat as sausage links.

"Wait here. I'll get Leda," he said and disappeared down the dark hall to the back.

I paced the entranceway, barely able to keep in my excitement. If the girl, Leda, was indeed the one from the pictures, how could I be sure? Was such a thing even possible?

"It couldn't be," I muttered under my breath.

For the first time, it occurred to me to do the math. If the picture had been taken between the early 1900s and 20s, that would make Leda over a hundred years old. She didn't look a day over twenty-five.

Minutes later, I glanced at my watch, then resumed my pacing, my eyes pasted on the dark hall up ahead. Heavy footsteps sounded in the distance. Claudio appeared at the end of the hallway; his silhouette lightened as he neared. He carried a large Styrofoam cup, a plastic dome lid on the top. He paused, took a sip through a straw, cocked his head, and studied me.

"Are you black or what?"

"Excuse me? What does that have to do with anything?"

He waved his hand as if that would dismiss the subject. "I was only curious."

"I was curious about your place on the human evolutionary ladder, but I was courteous enough not to ask."

Claudio rolled his eyes and took another long sip of his drink. He patted his chest and rattled out an even longer belch.

"Come on back," he rasped.

He led the way, his form filling the hallway as he lumbered along. I could hardly see where I was going as my eyes adjusted to the darkness. The hall bent to the right, and there were suddenly naked bulbs above us. They gave off a faint glow. Partially faded, old wallpaper adorned the walls. Chrysanthemums on a leafy background.

Doors, almost invisible, as they too were covered in the same wallpaper, were marked only by small knobs. I could barely make out their outlines. As we passed, I counted five. Up ahead, the hall bent left, but Claudio didn't take me that far.

He stopped at the fourth door and opened it.

I peered in and saw a room no bigger than a closet, with a chair in front of what looked to be a tall, narrow screen.

"Well, go in," he told me.

I studied him. In the light, his skin was remarkably smooth, hairless, his jowls as heavy as Atlas's. I peered back into the closet-like room and wondered if it would be the scene of my undoing. Claudio could push me in there, strangle me, and no one would be the wiser.

He eyed me back impatiently. "If you're having second thoughts, I don't give refunds."

I took a breath and entered. He closed the door behind me. I spun around in complete darkness. I made my way to the chair and placed my satchel at my feet.

I heard the mechanical whir of tiny motors. A thin horizontal beam of light appeared in the vicinity of the screen in front of me.

The light grew as the screen lifted to reveal a pane of one-way glass.

It was like peering backward through time. Beyond the glass sat a full-sized antique bed with a frame of metal in the shape of curling vines. Next to the bed stood a privacy screen painted with birds. A wooden stand affixed with a mirror held a washbasin and a pitcher. The same wallpaper from the hall covered the walls of the room.

She stood next to a closed door in a wraparound coat that came to her knees and a cloche hat covering her eyes. Her arms were crossed in front of her, and thin, pale hands clutched the lapels of the coat. She waited, still, as if she were posing.

I felt the hairs on my arms and the back of my neck stand on end. This was not like looking through time, I decided. It was like looking at one of the postcards hidden away in my rolltop desk, and it coming to life in my hands. I felt my breath hitch in my chest and realized I had been holding air in my lungs since the screen lifted. I turned my attention back to the scene beyond the glass and waited.

Slowly, she began to move. She opened her coat, revealing a slinky, champagne-colored dress. She hung the coat on a hook mounted to the door and walked forward, the hat still covering her eyes. She stopped in front of the basin and bent to peer at her reflection in the mirror. She removed the hat and tossed it on the bed.

For the first time, I got a clear view of her face and saw the heavy-lidded eyes, the long, straight nose and full lips. Her hair was dark and cut short, with straight bangs.

On the other side of the glass, Leda slowly straightened. She turned and stepped close to the bed, raised one leg, and put her foot on the bed. The hem of the dress fell back to reveal a rolled stocking nearly the same color as her flesh, held on by a garter. On her foot she wore a stout-heeled shoe with a strap. She undid the buckles and slipped off the shoe, which she unceremoniously tossed on the other side of the bed.

She then slid off the garter and rolled the stocking down over her short, shapely leg. She straightened, turned, and sat on the bed. She brought up her other leg and undressed it of shoe, garter, and stocking.

Not once did she look at the glass that I sat behind watching her. I wished I would have brought one of the postcards, as I doubted my own eyes. It was the strangeness of the situation, the antiques and the clothes, all the artifacts of the past, one of my postcards come to life. I felt dazed, drugged, and my heart beat so fast I felt as if its clamor could compel my spirit to rise out of my body and float away.

In the room, Leda pulled the dress over her head. Beneath, she wore a chemise just a shade paler than her skin, and beneath that, through the one-way glass, I could see the pink of her nipples. Once again the breath seized in my lungs.

Leda returned to the basin and removed a sponge and a vial. She poured a bit of the vial's contents into the basin. She then retrieved the pitcher and poured water into the basin and used the sponge to stir it.

She gathered the chemise at the waist and lifted it over her head. She turned her back to the glass to reveal a myriad of tattoos. There was a hazard trefoil in the shape of a heart on her wrist. In the middle of her back, stretching from the base of her spine to her buttocks, was the Hanged Man from the tarot, bound upside down by one leg and clutching two small sacks. On her right shoulder was something written in what looked to be Aramaic script, and on her left buttock, a bunch of chrysanthemums that trailed up her side to her ribs.

I felt a pang of disgust. To me, tattoos were vile, the art of the ignorant, and I hated that Leda had possibly ruined her once-flawless skin with them. I put the thought in check as a clue that this could not possibly be the same girl. Leda was of this generation all right.

At the basin, she dipped the sponge into the water, brought it to her stomach, and began to bathe herself. The water dripped down her hips and between her thighs in clear rivulets.

In the mirror, I could see one of her breasts, small and pert, and tipped with an almost translucent pink nipple. I felt the glass under my palm. Without noticing, I had leaned forward so close that my breath fogged the glass in short puffs that disappeared as they made their mark.

Leda reached behind her and wiped the small of her back and below. The sponge left the area beaded with water, and the roses on her ass looked as if they shone with dew. She looked over her shoulder, right at the glass, then away again.

I sucked in an anticipatory breath and watched the woman on the other side of the glass turn completely around. There were more tattoos, a black widow spider beneath her navel, a red feather between her breasts. The hair over her sex had been trimmed down to a single strip on her mons in a pornographic style, not at all like the girls in my postcards. Still, I could have sat there long into the night watching Leda's birdbath.

She left the basin and went to the bed. She climbed onto the mattress and kneeled. Her legs parted, revealing the dark reddish-pink of her secret place. She began to sway slowly as if to some unheard music. As she did, she caressed her small breasts with her hands.

I gripped the armrests, felt that they were threadbare, and knew I was not the first to hold on tightly to them, to hold my breath there in that room. The thought of someone else sitting there in my place, watching Leda's show caused the contents of my stomach to slosh uncomfortably.

On the other side of the glass, Leda's hands traveled down her sides to her hips. She brought the fingers of one hand to her mouth and wet them. I could almost hear the sigh escape her lips and somehow travel through the partition to my ear. In one smooth movement, Leda bent backward, while her wet hand slid down between her breasts and over her stomach and parted the folds of her sex. The stretched skin at her pelvis rippled as her fingers played in the slick pink beyond the folds.

My face flushed hot. This could not possibly be right. I was a long way from my pristine little secret room and sanctuary. It felt unholy, an upside-down pentacle, a mass chanted backward. Live pornography for men like Jimmy and Claudio, who, I realized, was nothing but a glorified pimp. How he had taken my money with such glee.

A blunt force overtook my body. I doubled over, the beast suddenly upon me without any warning. I fell to my knees still gripping the chair, fighting the change. A groan tried to escape my body, but I held it down my throat where it pulsed like water in a plugged geyser. Through my narrowed eyes, I watched as Leda continued with her show, her fingers teasing deep.

At the sight of this display, the beast seemed to surge forward, challenging what little control I had left. I stood on rubbery legs, leaning on the chair, which toppled under my shifting weight. I shouldered a dark wall to support myself. My entire body ached from the threat of the change. The muscles in my jaw spasmed as I clenched my teeth from the effort of fighting back the beast.

I groped through the semi-darkness and fumbled at the door until my hand found the cool, metal knob. The soft light from the hall flooded the small space, and the beast faded back fast. When I realized my error, I looked over my shoulder to see Leda upright on the bed staring straight at me.

I slipped through the door and quickly made my way to the exit. As I reached the podium, Claudio stepped out of nowhere to block the way.

"Where are you going? The show ain't over."

I moved to go around, and his bulk sailed in front of me, blocking the path out.

"There's been an emergency at work…" I doubled over with the pain of the transformation. "I must go."

"No refunds," he barked.

"Fine."

"You a fucking cop?" he asked. "You a fucking narc?"

I sank to the floor, knees first. This could not be happening. I should have stayed at home and waited for Sandra to return and pamper me. She seemed a lifetime away now.

Claudio put a meaty hand on my shoulder. "What the fuck is wrong with you?"

A throaty growl escaped me. It gave me strength enough to stand on my own two feet. My shoes had split from their soles. The black claws curved from the hairy sinew at the cuffs of my pants.

Claudio stepped away from me. There was fear in his eyes, but he did not flee.

He began to change.

A black mist began to rise from his shoulders in swirling tendrils. Claudio threw his head back and the same shadowy fog rolled between his lips and down his chin. The mist solidified as it curled around his body giving it a different shape.

Not wanting to stick around to see his new form, I tried to scramble past. He lunged, and we bowled into a wooden-paneled wall. He pinned me to the floor, his beard a mass of vines, grass, and root-like protrusions. The smell of earth and decayed plant life was just as overpowering as his brute strength. His eyes were dark caverns in the rocky slope of his forehead. Nothing human remained.

He tangled his short, gnarled fingers into the patches of fur at my shoulders and rose to his bark-covered feet, taking me with him. Thick vines extended from his sides, snaking up, winding around my chest and back, binding my arms close.

The new appendages tightened with the swiftness of a noose. In a wheezing gasp, my lungs squeezed the air they held out of my muzzle. I struggled in vain, my clawed feet shredding organic debris from his body.

"Claudio."

The command came in a voice slightly louder than a whisper, deep and smoky, but definitely female. Our horned heads turned together in the voice's direction.

Leda stood wrapped only in a short, flimsy robe.

"What the fuck is going on?" she asked.

Claudio tightened his grip, and a pitiful whine escaped me.

Leda stepped forward. "Drop her. Now."

The vines slid away and I fell to the floor, human again, my clothes in near tatters. I drew my knees to my chest and wrapped my arms around my legs in an effort to cover myself. My eyes were glued on the girl from my postcards, alive and in color. Speaking to me.

"Who sent you?"

"Jimmy," I stammered.

She took a step forward, puzzled. "The goat man?"

"He showed me the flyer," I said.

She moved closer and stooped, placing a warm hand on my shoulder. Leda's eyes were an extraordinary shade of violet, more on the red spectrum than blue.

"Can you stand?"

Slowly, gingerly, I got to my feet.

"What's your name?"

I hesitated.

"Maybe if Claudio asks, you'll tell him."

He took a step forward and gave an unnatural growl. I had been so enrapt with Leda that Claudio's presence was forgotten.

"Tinsley Swan," I blurted, offering a small smile.

Claudio chuckled, a whispery sound like water grass in the wind. I shrank away from him, expecting him to attack me again.

"You shouldn't be afraid of him," Leda said. "He is only a leshy. You, my friend, are a dragon among dogs."

To illustrate her point, she whipped her head toward him.

"Get the fuck out of here," she said scathingly. "I don't want to see you until you're presentable."

With the tortured groan of a falling tree, Claudio stumbled off, his gnarled limbs swaying with each step. Clumps of sod fell to the floor as he went. Leda regarded the clods with a crinkled nose, as if they were the most disgusting thing she had ever encountered.

"Dumb animal," she said and reached out her hand. "Come to the back. I can get you some clothes, and while we wait, there are things we must discuss."

I hesitated, afraid to touch her.

She laughed and our eyes met. She snatched my hand and I gasped at the contact of warm, dry, soft skin instead of… whatever my imagination anticipated. Her fingers were strong around mine.

"There," she said, pulling me along. I followed, clutching my torn shirt with my free hand. She took me down the dim hall, and we turned to a large room with a beaded curtain instead of a door. The room was crammed with low couches and a bar where two women in their twenties sat on stools smoking from a hookah.

"Rose, bring tea," Leda said. "Snow Geisha."

One of the girls hopped off the stool and walked behind the bar.

We passed through the area and stopped at a door that Leda opened to reveal a smaller room with a patio beyond several panes of glass. I followed her inside and scanned the space. There were shelves, a desk in the Art Deco style detailed in various shades of wood, and several overstuffed chairs. My eyes fell on what looked to be a round bed covered in pillows of various shapes and sizes, and I deigned to speculate on what happened there.

I sat on one of the chairs and watched a smirk creep onto Leda's lips. She sat across from me, sinking low in the chair as she regarded me with eyes familiar to me through photographs decades old.

"How is it that you have what is mine, Tinsley Swan?"

"The beast, you mean," I said.

"Yes, my familiar," she answered.

"It's not by choice. This curse was forced on to me by my mother's family. The Tinsleys. I am named after them."

She shook her head. "I don't know any Tinsleys. I do know the woman who robbed me of my power…You carry her blood. I smell it."

My heart doubled its pace. That explained everything. Leda was a vampire, and here I was in her clutches, weak from the transformation, as if I could hope to escape the undead after a good night's sleep and a hearty breakfast.

"Alexandrine," I gulped.

The door opened, and the girl Leda had called Rose entered. She couldn't have been more than twenty in appearance, but I doubted my own eyes. She had caramel-colored skin and wore knee-high leather boots and a very short tunic dress. She carried a silver tray with an English tea service clattering lightly as she went. She threw me a lascivious grin before turning her attention to Leda.

"What happened to her clothes?"

"She met Claudio's other side," Leda said.

"No shit," Rose said blandly and set the tray on a low table. "And she lived." Leda crossed her legs, revealing a stretch of skin at her inner thigh.

"She's special."

Rose gave a short hum of approval and began to pour tea. "Sugar? Milk?"

I told her I wanted lots of sugar and no milk. She stirred two heaping spoonfuls and handed me a saucer with a small steaming cup. I sipped at it, not minding that I burned my tongue. Perhaps the sensation would wake me from this dream.

"She's going to need clothes for the party tonight," Leda said as she received a similar cup from Rose. "Tell Pearl to come look at her and you two can collaborate."

"Fine," Rose said and left.

We sipped our tea and watched each other.

"What is a leshy?" I asked. "You called Claudio that."

She grinned. "Very old. Very Slavic. A wood spirit that can take the form of a man."

I frowned. "He's not a man."

She sipped her tea. "We do what we can to survive."

The next question fell from my lips before I could stop it. "And you?"

"Like you, I am cursed," Leda said simply. "Alexandrine cursed me to take a physical form every seventy years and be ritually murdered."

She spat the last word out with a staunch severity. My hands began to tremble as my thoughts were claimed by visions of the great pyre.

"What are you?" I asked.

"You know exactly what I am, Tinsley Swan," she said in a bored tone. "You carry what is mine, and you have the blood of Alexandrine in your veins."

"I didn't want any of this," I told her. "They forced it on me before I was old enough to know better—"

"It is an honor to carry the familiar."

"It ruined my life."

Leda smirked into her teacup. "So that's your issue. You feel as if you could not live your life freely because of the responsibility of the familiar."

I squinted at a sudden dull ache between my eyes. "What is this? Therapy?"

"It could be an enhancement to your life," Leda said. "If you'd allow it."

"An enhancement?"

"I'm sure you've noticed, especially during this cycle," she said. "Are you not stronger? Faster? More passionate?"

I thought of Sandra. I would normally never take a lover so close to the time of the transformation.

"Are you suggesting that I have super powers?"

She laughed at the sentiment. "Where do you think all those stories come from? They're passed in the blood."

"You speak a lot of blood."

"Do I?"

"What are you?" I asked again.

She grinned. We said nothing for a few moments.

"You're immortal," I said.

"Not exactly," Leda said. "My life, as you describe it, is not my own. It belongs to Alexandrine's little cult. Your people have me hostage."

I balanced my saucer and cup between my knees. "If you're not immortal, then why do I have pictures of you from the turn of the century?"

She smiled. "I suppose I was photographed in my last incarnation."

"My uncle knew you. His name was Charles. His brother was Malcolm. He told me that he met you in New Orleans and brought you to my family's home in Galveston. He said you disappeared, that he and his brother suspected foul play."

She set her own saucer aside. "I don't remember much of my past incarnations. Bits here and there."

"Do you always pose for pictures when you come back?" I asked.

"This body is a lovely prison, isn't it?" She stood, unbelted her robe, and let it fall open. "It helps me in my short journey. Men want to take my pictures, and women want to serve me."

A discreet knock came from the other side of the door, and Rose returned with a curvaceous blonde. The two leaned into each other and spoke softly, occasionally throwing glances my way. Leda stood and walked to the window. Her skin seemed to take on the glow of the fading sun. The silhouette of her body played through the flimsy fabric of the robe, more erotic than her little show behind one-way glass.

The girls left us alone again. I cleared my throat.

"You still haven't told me what you are."

Leda turned away from me and walked to the window. "I have been called many names over the years—Kali, Astarte, Hecate, the Oracle at Delphi, the Whore of Babylon, the devil's bride."

With each name she spoke, my heart beat a little quicker. She belted her robe and turned back to me, quickly crossing the space between us. When she reached me, she bent and placed her hand above my right breast, her skin hot through my torn shirt.

"My consciousness is older than time," she said. Was that even possible? I challenged myself to look up and into her eyes. When I did, I saw that her pupils had shrunk to specks, the violet of her irises inhumanly large.

"You're frightened of me," she said.

I nodded dumbly.

She reached up, and her hand landed gingerly on the side of my face. "There were once many of us. We fought and loved. Some of us rebelled for reasons I do not remember. One faction made the physical world, constrained by time, flesh, and bone to punish the others."

As she spoke, she caressed my cheek, and a lovely tingle

spread from the hollow space behind my ear to my ribs. My face flushed and Leda smiled slightly at the effect of her touch.

"I was on the losing side. I was jailed in the new physical world with many others. Some of us made the best of our squalor. We fell quickly into the trappings of the senses. We were trying to emulate the sensations of our divinity."

I pulled away from her touch. "So the world is the result of punished immortals?"

Leda scoffed. "The world. Mortal. Immortal. You speak in such limited terms, Tinsley. Your cult should have taught you better."

I looked up at her. "I am not part of a cult. I never was."

She raised her eyebrows. "You bear Alexandrine's mark."

"Not by choice." I moved to stand, but Leda sank forward, planted a knee on the chair between mine, and balanced herself there, arms at her sides.

"My own mother and aunt tricked me," I told her. "They put a mask on my face and forced me to become the beast."

Leda gasped. "Yes, the mask. That is how they stole away my familiar."

"Alexandrine?"

"Yes," Leda said and placed her palms on my shoulders. Her proximity charged the air between us into a hum as if charged by volts of electricity. "The spark burned bright in her. She called me from obscurity. She seduced me."

"Um, spark?"

"Every soul is a bit of that original fire," Leda said. "Mine burns bright, while yours is much brighter than your friend the goat man, and his has more glow than most."

She straightened and moved back to her own chair. "The worst punishment of all was watching our seed degenerate into disgrace. At first, we left them to their own devices, but the spark within them caused them to seek us out, and so we came to our long-lost children and civilized them. We discovered that their love gave us power."

"Religion," I said.

"Yes," she said. "It is not a one-way street, this love and power, but it can become…" She paused, searching for a word. "Muddled."

"Of course that didn't stop any of you."

"No," she said. "Of course that was ages ago." She laughed. "It gave us something to do with ourselves, to become just what our children wanted of us, demons, angels, gods."

"Immortals," I said, determined to make my point.

"No," she said. "We simply know how to hold on to what is left of our fire. The spark in the average human is so dim, it burns out quickly."

"And then what?" I asked. "When it burns out?"

She shrugged. "I only know the in-between place. The abyss. It is where I go when I am not in a physical incarnation."

"So how do you hold on to your fire?" I asked. "By drinking blood?"

Leda rolled her eyes. "You know better than that, Tinsley Swan." She sighed. "There are some who get pleasure from the spilling of blood and death, and chaos."

"And you?" I asked boldly. "How do you get your pleasure?"

She threw back her head and laughed. "By being a horny little freak, of course."

I shrank in my seat.

"So you've denied yourself because of my familiar?" she asked.

"Someone I cared about was hurt by the beast," I told her. "That cannot happen again."

She leaned forward. "Tell me."

"There was a girl in the Sisterhood, Alexandrine's cult," I

said. "We were both to be initiated. We fell in love, I suppose, the way young girls fall."

Leda nodded. "Sounds beautiful."

"I don't remember much of what happened," I said and touched the tattooed part of my chest. "They put a mask on me and I became the beast. I mauled her. What is it exactly?"

Leda pursed her lips. "My familiar is an extension of myself, a bit of my fire, my child."

I sighed. "I'm sorry it was taken from you."

"And the Sisterhood?" she asked. "Would they agree?"

"Of course not," I said. "They're looking for you—"

She waved her hand. "The Sisterhood cannot touch me tonight. You'll come out with me. I'm throwing a party."

"I should get home," I said. "Sandra will be worried."

Leda grinned wryly. "Sandra? I thought you were living like a monk."

I grinned back. "She's special."

My thoughts strayed to Sandra. What would she think of this half-naked woman who at least appeared to be young, so close to me? Sure, she could wrap her mind around finding me hiding in the bathroom at our workplace in the form of a beast, but could she fathom my seduction at the hands of this living, breathing goddess?

The door opened again, and a third girl, a lithe brunette with doe eyes, brought my satchel. I made a quick call to Sandra, who was of course worried about my whereabouts. I told her I was with Juliette, hearing her out. The lie came out so easily. I assured her that I could handle the meeting on my own, that I would see her the next morning at the weekly meeting.

My eyes were on Leda throughout the entire conversation, and, sitting cross-legged in her chair, she watched me as well, her violet eyes glimmering in the darkened room.

CHAPTER SEVEN

Leda left me in the hands of her girls to be coiffed and dressed. The outfit, I would have never picked out for myself in a million years. The pants were skintight, of a black, silky material that tapered at the leg. There was also a white, tuxedo style jacket, the lapels trimmed in the same material as the pants.

Pearl put some kind of foam in my hair and combed it into a pompadour much like Professor Swiggleslock.

"I look ridiculous," I said once they were finished with me.

"It's better than that high school math teacher vibe you were giving off," Rose snapped as she fussed with her own ebony tresses in the small dressing room mirror.

Pearl laughed at the barb. "I'm going to drink everything tonight."

"Leda's parties are always the most," Rose said.

They continued with the same mindless chatter as they disrobed right there in front of me and redressed in the skimpiest dresses and highest heels. We all filed out to the front of Little Foxes where Claudio waited in human form dressed in jeans, cowboy boots, and a Western-style shirt. He smirked at me and gave a nod.

Night had fallen outside, the surrounding businesses closed for the day. Next to the curb, a white vintage Rolls waited with Leda in the backseat, her hair a halo of white-blond curls, a horned headdress over them. Claudio moved to open the door for me, but I quickly crossed the distance and pulled the handle myself.

I slid into the backseat and openly stared. For a few miserable seconds, my heart refused to beat. Leda wore the exact same costume from the picture I had stared at for over thirty years. She was the Golden Goddess, her face serene save for that slight smile. Her body was clad in sheer silk, silver and gold, her breasts bare beneath. She leaned forward. The gold halo of the headdress caught and refracted the headlights of a passing car.

"How?" I asked.

She grinned. "How what?"

"I have a picture of you in this costume."

The Rolls began to move, piloted by Claudio.

"That is possible," Leda said. "It is one of my favorites."

"Do you always allow yourself to be photographed?" I asked.

"I allow myself to be worshipped, yes," Leda said. "Were you not paying attention?"

She placed my hand on her thigh. Her skin felt hot through the sheer material. "All these years, you've been watching me, haven't you?"

I nodded dumbly, not sure what to think or do, except kiss her. Which I did not, certain that I should be faithful to what Sandra and I had. Still, I didn't reclaim that hand. Leda closed her eyes and parted her lips.

Leda slid my hand higher until my fingers brushed her other thigh. Her lids fluttered open, and she laughed, placing my hand in my lap.

"Your Sandra is very lucky," she said decisively.

The Rolls slowed as we pulled in front of a procession of cars. I looked out the window to see the old bank on Washington Avenue, its neoclassical behemoth of a façade lit up with a pink spotlight.

A group of people reveled out front, and I realized they were waiting for us, for Leda. I looked to her, and she gave an exasperated sigh.

"I'm working tonight. This is a party for the Bacchanista thing."

I smirked. "Will Bacchus himself be there?"

"In spirit, I'm sure."

When we exited the car, the crowd gasped collectively, and some of them actually applauded. A few of them reached out to touch her as we passed. I clutched her hand, stunned by their rapt, awed faces. They called out to Leda, and she engaged them like a starlet, stopping to pose for pictures and exchanging clever banter.

"You're famous," I whispered.

Jimmy came to greet us as we entered the building. Leda kissed his cheek. "St. James," she said. "It seems we have a mutual friend."

"Tinsley?" he said.

Leda patted his arm and walked into a throng of partygoers.

"It seems she likes you," Jimmy said when she was out of earshot.

"Yeah," I said simply. "It seems she does."

He studied me, as if for the first time. "I never thought you would fit in with her crowd."

"And what exactly is her crowd?"

"Modern-day witches, neopagans, artists, misfits." He gestured to his broken body. "People who don't fit in with the rest of society."

"What makes you think I fit in?" I asked.

"Because you're so fucking straight-laced," he said and put an arm around my shoulders.

He trailed us as Leda took me around to introduce me to everyone. Many of the partygoers she had helped in some way.

She backed their businesses, provided them with a place to crash, a shoulder to cry on, and inspiration. From what I gathered, she just showed up in the community a year ago and started helping people.

A transgender woman in a sparkling pink dress called Leda her muse. A young man with a glass eye introduced himself as the brains behind the Bacchanista ads. I gave him my OddDuck card and told him to give me a call soon.

A local string quartet I like provided the music. They were joined by a stunning full-figured woman with a powerful voice who began to sing a bluesy song to their usual gothic score. Most of the evening was spent drinking and reveling. I danced with each one of Leda's witch-nymphs.

A little after midnight, Leda stood and whispered into my ear. "Now the real fun begins."

I moved to follow her, but she motioned for me to stay. Someone passed me a cigar with a fragrant smoke wafting from the end. I took a puff of it. The smoke coated my lungs, and I exhaled as a pleasant, light-headed feeling claimed me.

I wandered the room a bit. A bunch of people were gathered around a large gilded fish tank guarded by several men. Inside the tank, a woman lounged, her elbows resting on the rim, her dark hair damp on her shoulders. Her legs lay inside the tank covered by a tail of what looked to be stylized scales of shining blues and greens.

I said hello and tried not to stare as I wondered if she were some exotic form of entertainment or an eccentric who showed up at parties in a mermaid costume. She looked through me listlessly, and after a few seconds, she dropped her arms and sank into the water. There was not much room in the tank, an inch or so from her head to tail. She floated with her arms at her sides. She scowled and her face changed for a second. Her large eyes became glistening pools of black, her lips parted in a snarl to revealing two rows of conical teeth.

I gasped and stepped away, then looked to the men, but they were as stoic as the Queen's Guard. I noticed Jimmy approaching slowly in his hitching gate.

"That woman in the tank," I said. "She's not human, is she?"

"You're bound to see anything at one of Leda's parties," he explained.

"And those young women at Little Foxes?"

"Her coven," he said. "Leda's a witch."

"Is that so?" I asked.

He raised his eyebrows. "Claudio told me that you change. What's that all about?"

A commotion took over, and everyone craned their heads in one direction. I turned and saw Leda covered in nothing but lacy scarves, her arms and legs bare. The quartet stopped their song cold and began to play a slow, deliberate, overwrought march-like rhythm with their strings.

Leda began to dance, an exaggerated sway of her hips. She raised her arms and removed the scarf that covered her head. She lifted her leg and balanced on the toes of the other with the grace of a trained ballerina and untied a red scarf from around her ankle. The march sped up into a wild, gypsy-like folk tune, and her sway became more vigorous as she removed another scarf from her neck. Each scarf fell into the same pile and seemed to be the center of her movement.

Whatever I had toked on—I was sure it was marijuana—made my head swimmy. I tried to blink away the bleary feeling and saw Leda in a much different setting than the plush hall. In a lightning flash, I saw her on the muddy bank of a bayou, dark water rushing over the bottom half of her body, meeting with long, black hair.

She was cold, naked, and frightened. She crawled onto flat land beneath a freeway underpass and tilted her head beneath an icy stream of runoff that splashed from above. She drank, then used her hands to sluice away the mud. She smelled smoke and wandered to a camp of homeless old women gathered around a long-dead fire. They regarded her with rheumy eyes and chattered expletives at her nakedness.

The cold fire of wet bits of wood and debris sparked into a roaring blaze. The old women startled, and some of them ran far into the cold night. The ones who stayed watched as Leda walked into the fire, her feet among the now-burning trash. She squatted among the hissing flames for a moment, her skin glowing.

When she stood and walked out of the blaze, one of the old women stepped forward with a pile of clothes. She dressed Leda and received a kiss for her generosity.

I blinked again and found myself leaning heavily against a stool. The blackened edges of my vision cleared. I saw Leda, dancing. She sank to the floor as her upper body slithered like a snake. Away came the veil that covered her breasts, and the third, around her forehead. A collective gasp and applause followed. Only her waist and hip covered, Leda alternately swayed and posed, then spun madly and threw herself dramatically to the floor into a feral crawl. She left her pile of scarves. The music slowed again, now a mix between the paced plucking and erratic strums. The crowd parted for her.

I moved with them and Leda changed direction to follow my path. As she danced closer to me, she shed the veil around her waist, revealing her tattooed midriff, drawing gasps from the partygoers.

She moved close, swaying her hips. I felt her heat through my clothes, and it felt a lot like the pyre in '83. I glanced nervously around me. This was a hall full of people, not my secret room tucked away in my house behind a wrought iron fence. Jimmy stepped into my view, grinning, with a camera phone in hand, and I felt truly embarrassed. Leda caught my gaze, and her eyes changed, from cool violet to molten gold. She began to dance backward, and I moved with her. I glanced down at my wrist and noticed that she had tied the last scarf around it, and the other end was tied around her waist.

My eyes roamed low on their own behest. A scrap of red lace covered the V between her legs. A new tattoo glowed above her right breast; the seven-sided star glimmered like fire trapped beneath her skin. She ran a hand over the mark, and it brightened like stirred embers. With the same hand, she pointed at me, her finger aimed at my chest.

I tucked my chin and looked down at the mark above my breast. My own seven-sided star burned through the fabric of my jacket. She moved close to me again and wrapped an arm around my waist. She smelled of jasmine and sandalwood.

"I saw you," I said absentmindedly. "Like a dream while I was standing there just now."

"What did you see?"

"I saw you climbing out of the mud."

"You saw my birth into this incarnation," she whispered. "Each time, I hope it is the last, but then the Sisterhood catches me and burns me."

I moved to step away from her, but she held on to my waist and clutched the satin lapel of my jacket. The crowd seemed to shrink forward in some kind of anticipation.

"I shouldn't get involved—"

"Do you know how it feels to be burned?" she asked. "It's part of their cycle of ritual to burn me every seventy years. This body feels pain, Tinsley, and it hurts."

I looked down into her eyes, which had returned to their remarkable violet color, and they were teary. In my mind, I saw the Great Pyre burning, and in a split second, imagined a woman among the flames. I saw Leda among the roaring, hungry flames, heard her screams.

"Please," she said. "Don't let them burn me again."

She closed her eyes and rested her forehead against my breast. I realized that the partygoers still watched the two of us in an eerie breathless silence. I removed my jacket and draped it around her shoulders.

CHAPTER EIGHT

Before I opened my eyes the next morning, I knew the day would take a foul turn as soon as I ventured too far away from my bed. As soon as I sat up, my room became one of those terrible roadside fun houses. Leda's party had certainly lived up to its reputation, and before the night had ended, I was sure I saw old horned Bacchus laughing among the revelers.

Somehow, I ended up at home and in once piece, even though my head seemed to have been tampered with during the night. I stumbled to the bathroom hoping a cold shower would wake me.

When I stumbled back into my bedroom—a little more upright than before—my phone sang out Sandra's ringtone, the *Fame* theme song. I checked the time first. Ten thirty. I had missed the meeting. Perhaps Sandra was not mad, only worried.

I thumbed over the button to accept the call.

"Hello," I said attempting to sound chipper, though my tongue felt as if someone had run me over with a freight train.

"Where the fuck are you?" Sandra whispered harshly into the phone.

"At home," I said weakly. "I haven't been feeling well, you know."

"Cut the shit," Sandra said. "You weren't at home last night. Juliette and I deduced that."

My resolve crumbled along with my alibi. I tried to stammer out some kind of explanation, but Sandra hung up. I debated showing up for work after all. Perhaps it was best to stay away until the boss could cool off. Too bad the boss was also my lover and privy to some pretty heavy secrets, like my habit of turning into a beast.

I had lied, and ruined things with Sandra, all for a few cheap thrills with a young, beautiful woman. I collapsed back onto the bed.

"This is not the right time for a midlife crisis," I told myself.

Leda was so much more than a cheap thrill. I felt a profound connection with her, something that defied time and death. It was certainly something more than renting a U-Haul and taking an Alaskan cruise every other year.

I collected myself and dressed for the day in khaki linen pants and a white blouse. I drove the rental in to work. Once I reached the office, I entered cautiously. Bill Sands trailed me like an idiot, as he was in the main hall practicing on a mini putting green.

"She's pissed," he said. "I think she's been on the phone with Dallas all morning. She's in her office."

"I can handle it," I reassured him. I moved to go up the hall and he caught hold of my wrist, his face practically glowing beet red.

"There's a lady in your office," he whispered. "She told me not tell anyone."

"What?" I asked.

"She's young, and…" He swallowed. "She's got on this minidress thing."

Leda. I felt the blood drain away from my face. I hauled ass to my office and found her standing there in a neon pink clingy minidress and black ankle boots. Black sunglasses nested in her hair. She smiled when she saw me, and for the life of me, I smiled back.

She came close and kissed my cheeks European style. I turned and noticed that Bill watched us, amusement in his eyes.

"Good-bye, Bill," I said. "Don't tell Sandra I'm here."

He grinned and slipped out, closing the door behind him after waving at Leda. I didn't dare speculate about what he thought of Leda and what he would go tell the other Bill and their pals.

"What are you doing here?" I asked her as pleasantly as I could.

Leda chose to perch her cute ass on the edge of my desk with her legs crossed. "I came to see you, of course."

"Well, it might not be safe," I said. "The Sisterhood has been stalking me. I think they've figured out who you are. I led them to you."

Her slight smile quickly faded. "They would have found me, just like they did before."

I quickly paced to the door and made sure it was locked. "You should leave town."

She sighed and reached out her hands, and I stepped close to take them. "I have a plan, Tinsley, a way to free us both."

My knees weakened at the word *free*. Was it even possible? I thought of my life without the beast, perhaps with Sandra and the U-Haul and the Alaskan cruise.

"Come to me tonight and I'll tell you."

I nodded dumbly. She scooted off my desk and went for the door.

"Be careful," I said.

She smiled and left me.

I put my things away and then made my way to Sandra. She sat behind her desk with a grave look on her face as she listened to her phone.

"She's here now," she said. "We'll see you soon."

"Who was that?" I asked when she put her phone down.

"Juliette."

"Why are you talking to her?"

Sandra stood. "Because it's every Catholic girl's dream to save the world from the fabled end times."

"You can't believe anything she says," I said. "The Sisterhood is a cult, just like any other. They're thieves and murderers."

She frowned. "Who told you that? Your goddess?"

I narrowed my eyes. Juliette had ratted me out. She was using Sandra to get what she wanted out of me.

"She's not a goddess," I said, unsure of how I could tell her Leda's story. "Not the way you think anyway. She's scared."

Sandra sat and threw up her hands. "I suppose she needs you, the beast, to protect her?"

"Yes," I said. "She is cursed. Like me."

"Tinsley," Sandra said decisively. "You're coming with me to talk to Juliette, whether you like it or not."

I pondered the demand for a moment. "Yes, okay," I said. "As long as you're not mad at me."

"You lied to me," she said. "And then Juliette told me you found the Lost Goddess, that the beast led you to her."

"That's not true," I countered.

"Then why are you hiding her?"

It was a good question, and I didn't have the answer. "They bring her back to life just to burn her in the Sacred Fire. Why can't they just be rid of her if she's going to bring about the end of the world?"

Sandra shook her head. "How am I supposed to know how these things work? I'm just glad you're all right."

We both walked around the desk until we met in each other's arms. I couldn't help but compare holding her to having Leda close. Sandra felt more solid and safe. Dancing with Leda the night before felt as if I were holding a stick of dynamite.

She moved away. "Juliette wants us to meet her at Salacia."

"No," I said.

"She says there's something she has to show you," Sandra said. "And anyway, I'd like to see the legendary place."

I shot her a look. "You only know what I've told you." I frowned. "And what Juliette told you, the sow."

She raised a hand. "Let me give you something." She went behind her desk and opened a drawer. She returned with a small velvet sack. She opened it and turned the back over in her hand. A tangle of red string and silver charms fell onto her palm.

"Let me tie this around your wrist."

I smiled and obediently held out my arm. "What are they?"

"Milagros. They symbolize saints that answer certain prayers," she said as she fastened the red string. "A house is for safe travels, and loved ones at home. The arm is strength. The eyes are for insight and vigilance. The woman's head is for the safety of your spirit."

She touched each one as she named it, as if infusing it with the magic she described.

"This praying woman represents St. Rose of Lima. I was born on her saint's day." She looked up at me. "And this heart represents love, Tinsley."

"Thank you," I said, suddenly nervous in her gaze, not sure if I had it in me to return what she offered.

"It will protect you, I hope," she said.

I kissed her passionately. "When all this is over, can we pick up where we left off?"

She tilted her head. She stepped backward and waved me away when I tried to follow her.

"Go on, get something done. We're leaving soon."

"Fine," I said and went to my office. Once I was settled

behind my desk, my phone chirped letting me know I had a text message.

See you tonight@Foxxies

"God," I said. "How am I going to pull this off?"

❖

Later that afternoon, Sandra drove too fast down I-45 toward Galveston, singing in Spanish along with a smoky-voiced woman crooning an endless set of romantic ballads. I tapped my fingers on the door handle and stared out the window at the open fields of tall grass. In my other hand, I held the ring of keys that would open the iron gates of Salacia, the Tinsley family estate, and any door after that, including those carved with the seven-sided star.

"I don't know what other dirty secrets she could dredge up," I said. "We could have met in town. Hell, I would have invited her to my house and we could have talked over cocktails."

Sandra turned down her music and made a sympathetic face. "How long has it been since you've visited?"

"I go every year to check up on the work the caretaker does," I said. "My father insists I keep up the place just in case I ever want to put it on the market."

"So why haven't you sold it?"

I shrugged. "It seems wrong. The place is over two hundred years old, and the land itself has been in the Tinsleys' possession for much longer. They made their money running a sugar plantation, and yes, there were black Tinsleys who owned slaves."

"Wow," Sandra said.

"Degenerates, my father calls them," I said. "He says he knew, even before he married my mother, that the Tinsleys were tainted."

"But he married her anyway."

I turned to look out the window again. I didn't like to think about my mother, let alone talk about her.

"She was beautiful, and she came from old money, and my father was a ladder-climbing little upstart. She was his prize, and in the end, his biggest shame."

Sandra chuckled ruefully. "What happened that summer, Tinsley?"

"Everything went wrong. Everything."

"Tell me," Sandra said.

It was high summer. I was fourteen and practically on the edge of the passenger's seat of my mother's Mercedes. That day, at the end of June, she chain-smoked with the window down. I was always very interested in her when she smoked. She didn't look like my fussy, worried mother. She said the nicotine evened her out.

Cigarettes were a habit my father disdained, even more so if done publicly. He had strict guidelines of how my mother and I should appear in public. We were to always be impeccably groomed when we went out, especially if he came along.

My mother was a mystery to me, and I only felt I caught glimpses of her true self when she was away from my father. She had more edge. She said "damn" and "hell." She was beautiful. Her hair was redder than mine and flowed down her back. She was glamorously slender. We had the same skin, toasted ginger. I liked being out with her, seeing the looks she received from men of all colors. She handled her beauty like a great burden, and I, in turn, saw my own blooming beauty as a monstrous responsibility.

That day, we were on our way to Salacia, the estate of her family, the Tinsleys. My aunt Quinn lived there, and I was to spend the summer with her. I had only met Quinn once, at my seventh birthday party. She had given me sapphire earrings and my first bottle of perfume, something flowery she had purchased in Marrakesh. Perfect for a young girl, she had explained.

As my mother drove past a marshy field of tall grass, I thought of the previous seven years. I was no longer a little girl, and though I was certainly conscious of how far along in the distance womanhood waited, I knew it closer than ever.

"What is it, my little thinker?"

Mom was always sensitive to my moods. No one since had been able to read me quite like she could. As always, I told her what I thought she would like to hear.

"I've never been away from you."

"No, you haven't," she said. "This is a good thing, though. Aunt Quinn is very excited about spending time with you."

"Why did she never get married?" I asked.

My mother lit another cigarette, all the while watching me from her periphery. "Your father doesn't want you to know this, but Quinn doesn't care for the company of men."

I frowned. Who did?

My mother glanced from the road ahead to me and then back at the road again. A group of older kids flew by in an old station wagon, playing loud pop music. The car rattled loudly and belched a cloud of exhaust, but the chrome of the bumper sparkled in the sun with youthful abandon.

Mom spoke again, carefully, as if Dad were in the backseat. "Your aunt Quinn takes women as lovers, not men."

I felt my face flush as the faces of certain female school friends of mine plagued my brain. They were girls that I had strange stirrings for, feelings I should have had for boys at my age. I had desperately tried to smother these feelings for some time to no avail, and so I hid them away.

Mom grinned at me. "Well, there's no need to be embarrassed. It's just the way things are sometimes. Believe me; it's for the best. I don't want you to think that your only lot in life is as some rich man's wife."

I looked at my mother. Not sure what to say. She was talking to me as if I were a grown-up, and it made me uneasy. "You're a rich man's wife."

She puffed a short cloud of smoke out the window and chuckled. "Yes. I'm a good wife. It's a noble servitude. It was my destiny. But I knew the day you were born, you would have more."

My visit with Quinn took on a new meaning. My beautiful spinster aunt was suddenly my beautiful lesbian aunt who lived her life as she pleased. She would show me how to do the same. I decided I would tell her about those girls at school, the ones I sneaked sidelong looks at and daydreamed about kissing when I could bear to allow myself to. It all thrilled me, and being a timid child, it frightened me.

Salacia sat in the middle of a wide plot of land, flat and green with a few small copses of trees scattered about. The house itself looked much smaller from the main road, but as we drove closer, I could see the towering palms around the yard that barely cleared the roof. It was old and Southern with white columns and a veranda. My mother got out and opened the white wrought iron gate topped with tritons.

A narrow drive covered with white gravel led us to the front yard where a peacock and peahen strutted through the green grass. Aunt Quinn appeared in a red and orange strapless sundress, the hem trailing the ground behind her, and the front brushing the tops of her bare feet. Her hair was lighter and curlier than Mom's and rested on her shoulders. Her frame was slighter. She smiled when she saw me and rushed over to hug me.

"Is this our little Tinsley?" She kissed my cheek. "She's gorgeous."

"Please be patient with her," Mom said. "She's shy."

She sounded wary, almost anxious.

"Of course," Aunt Quinn said. I hadn't noticed, but she held my hand. "Well, it's time for Tinsley to see her family home."

She led the way with me in tow. Mom lagged behind as if she

were a guest and hadn't grown up in that grand old house. She stopped to hug a matronly Mexican woman called Lola who then hugged me.

Quinn showed us around the house like a docent and recited its history as we went.

"This site of the house is even older than the city. The original was torn down in 1856, and this one was built by your great-great-grandmother, Cornelia."

She led us past a sweeping foyer with marble floors and a winding staircase that separated two wings. A chandelier loomed over us, its crystal fixtures winking minute rainbows of light.

"The Tinsleys have never been very good with money." She grinned. "In the mid eighteen hundreds, we were ridiculously wealthy."

She showed us the parlor, the Victorian furniture, and the library with oak shelves that reached the ceiling. The shelves were lined with old leather-bound volumes with gold or silver lettering.

"Your uncle Charles practically lived in here. After he passed, I finally got it cleaned of all the bachelor germs." She smiled at me. "Your mother says you'll like this room the best."

She was right. The large, stuffy room was cramped with tables and shelves of objects. A glass cabinet full of curious objects captured my attention first. My fingers itched to handle the bounty before me; a feathered wooden pipe, a mask carved from black stone, and a sheriff's badge, among other things. There were some antique pieces from the Egyptomania period, a silver and gold sphinx clock, and matching jackal candlesticks.

"I do like this room," I said decidedly, and they laughed.

"Well, you're welcome to take any of these things home when you leave," Aunt Quinn said. "They're part of your inheritance."

"Oh Lord," Mom said. "She loves old things. Her room will look like an old man's study."

We passed through another hall and stopped at a large set of double doors with large brass handles. I reached out and touched the carvings, two large stars with seven points.

"That is a family crest of sorts," Aunt Quinn said next to me. "The great heptagon."

"What is this room?" I asked.

"The ballroom," she answered. "I will show it to you soon."

We had an old-fashioned tea for just the three of us, with sandwiches and lovely little cakes. The two of them laughed and talked of old times. They were beautiful together, and I wished for a sister to share things with. We went out to the back porch, and as the sun faded, they smoked cigarettes and chatted.

The time came when Mom announced that she had to go. Tears pooled in my eyes as I watched my mother and aunt hug, kiss, and say their good-byes. I blinked back my emotion, determined not to seem like a baby. I managed to hold myself together as I said good-bye to Mom. If she noticed the tears that threatened, she graciously ignored them. She kissed my forehead and roared away in the Mercedes, leaving the smell of her perfume and cigarette smoke in the air.

Aunt Quinn put an arm around my shoulders in the gathering darkness. "You're very brave, Tinsley."

I followed my aunt back inside the stately house and barely listened to her idle chatter about how stuffy it could get at night, about visiting the stables the next day and planning a ride into town. My thoughts were of home and my place in the passenger seat next to my mother, our own front yard, and our kitchen.

Aunt Quinn and I sat in the parlor and looked over old family albums. There were scenes around the house and at the beach mostly, but there were settings all over the country and the world. The pictures dated back over a hundred years.

I was surprised to find that women and girls were prevalent in the family. Aunt Quinn pointed out a school picture with her *and my mother, and a boy she claimed that she and my mother were both in love with.*

"Before I knew better," she said, as if she knew that I knew of her preferences.

She then asked me about school, if I had any friends, specifically boyfriends.

I blushed and shook my head.

"Girlfriends?"

I didn't have anything to say except: "That would be very hard."

Aunt Quinn laughed and sighed. "Yes, and it remains that way, until you can become independent of those who disapprove."

I shook my head. "I'll have to wait to think much about those things. I want to finish school and go study someplace far away. In England. Daddy doesn't approve, so I'll work hard to get a scholarship." I had never spoken of my true plans for the future with anyone. I often fanaticized about my life as a grown-up—successful, freed to go where I chose, and of course being with a woman.

Aunt Quinn smiled. "You're very wise, but life sometimes upsets our plans."

I hardly slept that night, being in a strange place, and my aunt's words plagued me. I slipped out of bed at dawn, dressed, and went down to the library. I perused stacks of books. One of the authors jumped out at me: Marquis De Sade. I had heard some girls at school talk about the word sadism *and how it came from a man who wrote horrifyingly perverted books. Curious, I opened the book. It was titled* Justine of the Misfortunes of Virtue *and it was about an orphaned young woman separated from her sister in seventeenth-century France. She tried to remain virtuous, but she fell into all sorts of traps, was raped and imprisoned.*

Disgusted, I put the book away. Several stiff sheets of

yellowed paper fell from the book to the dark, wooden floor. I noticed that they were pictures, and so I stooped to inspect them. They were old black-and-white pictures of women in various states of undress. Then there was the Golden Goddess, as I would come to call her. As I stared at the picture, the edges of the world around me seemed to darken. When I looked away, I wasn't sure how much time had passed. I replaced the pictures and wandered from the room still in a daze.

Aunt Quinn met me in the hallway, smiling. "There you are, poking around in that old library. Find anything interesting?"

"Lots of stuff," I told her, too embarrassed to go into detail.

We had breakfast together and then walked down a worn path laced at the sides with wild flowers. Quinn looked different, yet just as pretty in jeans and a Western shirt, her hair pulled back into a sandy, red-gold tail. I was excited to slip on my riding boots. I wanted to ride the open space of the estate and down to the beach.

Determined to prove how much I knew about horses, I talked about the work I usually did in the summers at the stable. It had been Daddy's idea that I learn the value of a dollar. So I worked at the stables where I took riding lessons. It was my hope that my father would reward me with my own horse. For years, I had known that we could certainly afford it. Buying a horse was what my father would call frivolous spending. So I answered the phones in the office and kept things tidy in the storeroom and tack room to prove how responsible I could be.

Aunt Quinn had two horses, a black Tennessee Walker named Nonios, and a sorrel mustang with a white blaze between his eyes she called Abatos, named for two of Hades' steeds. She was especially proud of the mustang because he had been born a feral horse, captured, and broken in Nevada.

"He's still practically wild," Aunt Quinn told me. "I got him just for you."

I grinned in disbelief. "Really?"

"Of course," she said. "It's time we spoiled you a bit. You are a Tinsley, after all."

I went to the horse and patted his muzzle. He was larger than any horse at the stables where I took lessons. He seemed overwhelmingly muscled, eager to flaunt his strength as he tossed his head and trotted away.

"We'll get him used to you," Aunt Quinn assured me in a half-scolding manner. "You'll have to learn to assert yourself. Once you tame a horse, women are a piece of cake."

I flushed at her talk. She showed me around the stables. There were ten stalls. She told me that once each held a horse.

"In better times," Aunt Quinn said bitterly. "When the money was plentiful."

"What happened?"

"Time," she answered. "But we have other riches in our family."

We saddled the horses and I climbed atop Abatos. The big horse fidgeted once I mounted him. I reined him in clumsily, scared of the big horse's genealogy. At the stable where I worked, we knew of each horse's sire and dam. The painted stallion, though, was a mystery, as wild and mysterious as his mythological namesake.

We rode side by side, and my heart swelled. This was the land the mysterious Tinsleys had lived on for over two hundred years. It seemed I was learning a new part of myself.

"You handle that horse well," Quinn said with a smile.

"You think so?" I asked. "He's a big horse."

Wildflowers weaved through the tall grass of the open field. We skirted around the occasional oak and their roots that twisted above the ground. I smiled when I heard the roar of the Gulf ahead.

"I want to show you something," Quinn said. She stopped her hose and dismounted. I followed suit. She took Abatos's reins

away from me and motioned to the tall grass ahead. I walked in the direction she pointed and noticed a white stone obelisk among the twisting vine with trumpet-shaped purple flowers. I pulled away the greenery and saw that words had been chiseled into the stone.

Here Alexandrine D'Orleans landed in 1786
Long Live the Sisterhood

Below was a carving of the seven-sided star. I wondered what it meant. I straightened and turned to Quinn. "Who is Alexandrine D'Orleans?"

"Our ancestor," she said. "She was a French noble who left her home and privileged life for a great cause."

"The Sisterhood?" I asked. "What is that?"

"Our legacy," Quinn told me.

She handed back the reins. "There is much I have to share with you, Tinsley."

I nodded, and as we walked, I waited for her to tell me about Alexandrine and the Sisterhood, but she remained silent. She watched me gallop through the surf and seemed pleased to watch me do so.

We returned to the house and had lunch. After that, we looked at more photographs in the parlor. The phone rang, and Aunt Quinn went to answer it in the other room. I heard her chatting excitedly in French. I picked up on a few phrases and found myself impressed with her fluency. After half an hour of listening to the talk and trying to catch the gist of the conversation, I closed the album in my lap and drifted to the library. After doing some serious poking around, I found a bottle of rum stashed in a hollowed-out old globe. I also found a case of beetles pinned down under glass. A corresponding book lay close by, full of exact little lithographs.

I went for my sketchbook and began to sketch the beetles

in studious detail using a wonderful old oak desk as my work area. I equipped it with a magnifying glass on a stand and a green-hooded lamp. I lost myself in drawing, truly pleased with my skills. I don't know how much time passed. I heard the door open and turned to see Quinn. She crossed the room to study my handiwork.

"Your mother said you're clever," Aunt Quinn said. I turned to see her standing behind me, gazing at my drawings.

She told me it was dinnertime, so I followed her to the dining room. We talked of Abatos and my hopes that my father would not see the gift as undermining his parenting.

"You must stop being frightened of your father," Quinn said. "He's only a man."

I didn't know what to make of such talk. Though not a fan of my father's denial of certain things, I was under the impression I would be a better person for it in the end. There were too many girls at school who were spoiled and reckless because their parents could afford it.

"I'm not afraid of my father. I only wish he wasn't so stuffy and that he didn't work so much."

Aunt Quinn looked at me with obvious pity.

"I'll talk to him first about the horse," I said. "Abatos is mine, a gift from my other family. I should be allowed to keep him."

Quinn smiled, obviously impressed. I returned to the library and my sketches until I could hardly keep my eyes open. Tired, I went upstairs to the wonderful claw foot tub in the bath that adjoined my room. As the tub filled with steaming water, I pinned up my hair. I stepped over the porcelain rim and sank into hot, clear water. The pipes made noises that startled me when I pulled the stopper from the drain.

"Just pipes," I said to myself and wondered if the old house was haunted. Someone had to have died there. I admonished myself for spooking myself like a little kid. I returned to my room dressed in my pajamas. A still figure in red startled me. It was Aunt Quinn standing statue still as she gazed down at a pile of my sketches. She wore a blood-red kimono embroidered with gold and silver cranes, alternating with orange and yellow peony. Her hair hung loose around her shoulders like a headdress. She glowed in the lamplight.

She looked up at me. "Come, Tinsley, there's something I must show you."

Quinn moved toward the door, turned, and saw the reluctance on my face. She came to me and took my hand. I followed her down the dimly lit hall. She seemed to float in the floor-length kimono; the only proof that she walked were the minute peeks of the balls of her bare feet. We went down the stairs past the library to the carved double doors of the ballroom.

From her sleeve she produced a key. She glanced at me as she fit the key just under the door handle. "This is your legacy, Tinsley."

She pushed the doors open, exposing a room lit with flickering lamps, their dim light revealing walls paneled in golden-colored, gleaming wood. The floors were the same, as was a circle of round, low stools covered in a plush red fabric.

The ballroom, though I did not see how anyone could dance in there, ended with a set of steps that led to a raised platform, all carpeted with a pattern of stars.

"This room is a chapel of sorts. It symbolizes the wisdom Alexandrine has passed down to us through the ages."

I paused in my step, shaken. Though my parents were not very religious (I couldn't see my father having faith in anything or anyone more than what he could accomplish with his own brain), I couldn't imagine people in modern times worshipping any other religion.

"Our beliefs are a gift that came to our ancestor in France, Alexandrine D'Orleans, years before anyone thought to call this continent under our feet a country," Aunt Quinn told me. "She started the Sisterhood, an opportunity for women to explore the true nature of the other realm, away from men and their lies."

She smiled at me and touched my face. "Your eyes are as huge as saucers."

"Is this for real?"

She chuckled softly. "The Sisterhood will come next week. Members from all over the world, as we do every seven years. It is my hope that you will join us."

I didn't know what to say. I walked past her and explored the room. On the floor at the center of the circle of seats was a large tile mosaic of a seven-sided star wreathed in fire.

"The great heptagon," Aunt Quinn said, touching my back. "The source of our power comes from seven, Tinsley. Being a member of the Sisterhood means that you cannot become a mother. We give you that choice. We invite new members from our family—nieces, cousins, friends."

"Does that mean Mom is not a member?"

"Our aunt Cornelia invited me," Quinn said. "Your mother was chosen to give us you, a true descendant of Alexandrine, the last."

She pointed in the distance, and I followed her finger to two paintings. One seemed to put the viewer at a high vantage point looking down at the small figures of seven hooded figures leading a pale, naked woman. The other was a portrait of a dark-haired woman. She wore a low-cut dress that must have been scandalous in her time. Being an amateur student of art, I noted that the picture was unlike any from its time. Alexandrine looked as if she had been painted on the move. Her dark tresses flowed behind her, right off the frame, brow bent, determination in her eyes. Her décolletage shadowed a book that she carried under her arm. Her eyes were fierce.

"Her line ends with you, Tinsley," Quinn said softly behind me. "I need you to accept."

"What do I need to do?" I asked without turning.

She came close behind me and took my hand. I turned to face her. Without a word, she pulled me to the platform. There was a low table with a heavy gold pitcher and two short glasses. Quinn poured what looked to be wine into each of the glasses.

"Drink."

I reached out, then hesitated.

"It's okay, Tinsley. Trust me."

I did. The wine was sweet. It warmed my stomach and calmed my nerves. My aunt downed her glass in one swallow. She used the sleeve of her kimono to wipe away the red rivulet that escaped the corner of her mouth.

"Now what?" I asked. My words suddenly had recoil and echoed inside my head. The dim light shrank into a tight circle around us, and the darkness beyond became as vast as space. My aunt stood. She had a twisted face in her hands, with angry, sideways apostrophes for eyes, a pointed chin, and a crown of seven horns. She walked toward me slowly.

Frightened of the face she held, I attempted to back away, scooting on my backside. The room tilted, and I ended up on my back, my aunt looming over me with that awful face. Someone whined like a wounded dog. It was me.

I squeezed my eyes shut and felt Quinn's weight on me. I felt something warm and leathery on my face, the bristle of a million stiff hairs. I knew that she was covering my face with that grotesque thing she carried in her hands.

She spoke my name. I opened my eyes and saw Quinn's face through a veil of horns. She opened her kimono, revealed her breasts and the seven-sided star over one of them. She leaned forward, placed her hands on my shoulders, and pinned me to the floor. Time passed. We both remained still, save our ragged breathing.

She braced her body, and I felt her full weight. My body suddenly bucked as if attempting to throw her off. I moved again, more violently than before; my neck whipped side to side. I felt *like a fault being ground between two opposing forces, one above and below.*

Quinn lay on top of me. I felt her breath on my neck. I blinked.

I was on my feet, and she was rolling away. I saw a swatch of skin like mine, alternating with red and gold and silver. I moved faster than I ever had. The room slanted violently, and I had crawled halfway up one of the wood-paneled walls.

Quinn moved in the darkness, her open kimono trailing the floor. She carried a crook in one hand and a flail in the other. Her arms were outstretched at her sides. Something inside me screamed that she meant to do battle.

I leapt on her, and we rolled. I clawed her with my nails. She raised the crook and belted me across the face. Fabric tore. One of us cried out. I ended up on my stomach with Quinn on top.

"You are strong, Tinsley," she said into my ear as she pulled that awful horned face away from mine—a mask, I realized.

She rose from me and walked away, into the darkness. I closed my eyes, and terrible dreams came. I saw the beast for the first time in the mists of my nightmares. It pursued me down the family beach, the deafening roar of the crashing waves segued into a different dream of a woman lashed to a stout wooden pole. It was night, and water ran over her feet as the world tilted side to side. She was lashed to the mast of a ship. Then there was a fire, a tall pyre, and a ring of women naked and singing. Cloaked in those flames was a burning woman. Her skin did not bubble or blister; it glowed. Her eyes were closed as if she slept serenely. She was the woman dressed in armor from the picture in the library.

I woke the next day, in bed. From the intensity of the sunlight that streamed through the window, I knew it was late. I scrambled out of bed, woozy from the previous night's ordeal and unsure exactly of what I had been through.

Aunt Quinn waited in the dining room before a row of silver, her hair tied back with a kerchief. She looked like my mother for a minute, especially when she smiled. "Tinsley, you're awake."

I frowned. "What happened last night?"

She waggled a gloved finger at me. "You can't hold your wine."

Lola appeared with a tray, grinning. She smiled at me as she set out tea and toast. "You should eat. Some food will settle your stomach."

I smiled back weakly and sat at the table, but glared at my aunt as soon as the maid's back was turned. "What did you tell her? That I got drunk last night?"

Quinn studied me for a moment. She reached over and began to prepare me a cup of tea. "You must learn to tell people what they can understand."

"Well, shouldn't I understand what happened?"

She sighed and set the cup in front of me. "You are a Sister of Flame now, an initiate of the Sisterhood. We have passed down a great wisdom through the generations, and we protect the secrets of that wisdom."

"And what's that?"

She picked up her task of polishing silver. "I have already spoken too much. All Mystai must be blind, and enter unknowing."

I took a bite of toast. I chewed and swallowed. "I want to go home."

Quinn rolled her eyes. "Don't be such a child."

"This is weird and sick."

She put down the silver. "Why? Because you saw my breasts? You have to let go of that Puritan shit and just follow my lead on this."

I flushed at her words and ducked my head. She covered my hand with one of hers.

"I can send you home if that's really what you want. Perhaps we did not do enough to prepare you for this day."

It took me some time to speak. I thought of the mask and the surge of energy I felt the night before. "It's magic, isn't it? The wisdom?"

She smiled. "It's more than magic."

I finished my tea and toast in the library. I found the copy of Justine *and the picture of the woman in armor. The night before, her image had surfaced to the top of my fevered dreams. She had spoken to me in a strange language. I closed my eyes there in the library and tried to remember more. Instead of the woman in armor, I saw a red sky glittering with stars, and a moon as dark as a black hole.*

Aunt Quinn left me to my own devices the next few days. She was preparing the house for her so-called sisters who were coming to visit in my honor. I tried to keep myself busy and not think about it. I sketched in the library and became acquainted with the Justine. *I rode Abatos down to the beach. At night, I took sips from the bottle of rum hidden in the globe in the library. I found a few sips soothed me and helped me sleep at night without dreams of that frightening horned face.*

One evening as I returned from a ride as the last light faded from the sky, I heard voices in the parlor. Curiosity won out over my shyness and so I entered the room to find Quinn sitting with a woman and a girl a few years older than me. They both had ebony skin and a cascade of woolly black hair down their backs, the older woman's loose, the girl's tied with a ribbon.

"Tinsley." My aunt stood and came over to me smiling. *"This is my good friend Sophie, and her niece, Juliette."*

She pulled me over to them, and they both kissed my cheeks and spoke in French. Their warmth embarrassed me, and I looked to my aunt for help.

"Go ahead and wash up," she said. *"We're going to have dinner."*

I did as told. On my way to the bathroom, I stopped at the library to have a taste of the unlabeled bottle. I showered, groomed, and went down to the dining room. On the way, I found Juliette standing before the great double doors of the ballroom. She touched the carvings, and something protective wanted me to tell her to stop. There were frightening things on the other side of that door.

"Tinsley," she said when she noticed me. "Your aunt says that you are Mystes now."

I nodded, not trusting myself to speak. Her accent was enchanting, and her dark eyes sparkled in the dim light of the hallway. She smiled and took my hand. The contact thrilled me.

"We will be initiates together," she said. "After the gathering, we will be Sisters."

"Isn't this all a little bit strange to you?"

She regarded me with the prettiest puzzlement. "Strange?"

"It's like a feminist cult that has existed all these years," I whispered. "Men never found out? The church?"

She laughed. "Sophie says that women have always had secrets, even those we must keep from certain members of our own sex."

"I suppose it's because I am an outsider," I said.

"You are not an outsider," Juliette said. "You are part of Alexandrine's bloodline, and that is important to the Sisterhood."

I nodded, taking in her words. She still held on to my hand, her soft grip strengthening as we stood there in the hallway talking.

"You must not doubt, Tinsley," she said. "There are members of the Sisterhood who doubt us because we are young."

"But I thought my heritage guaranteed I would be accepted."

"There are Sisters who do not believe young initiates should be trusted in these times. Quinn was not to initiate you on her own. It has caused quite a stir, Sophie says."

"She didn't tell me."

Juliette smiled. "You are her progeny, and she will protect you at all cost."

We heard footsteps and looked up to see Quinn at the end of the hall. She smiled.

"Juliette will coax you out of your shell yet."

I realized then that Juliette still held my hand. I pulled away and moved toward my aunt who just stood there grinning.

We ate supper in relative silence. I was unnerved, not sure what to do with myself or what to say, and it felt like school. Sophie asked me if I played any sports, and I told her that I rode horses. She then tried to test my French, and I struggled to keep up, especially when Juliette joined in.

After dinner, Sophie and Quinn excused themselves.

I went to the library. Juliette followed me. She marveled over the room and its curiosities. I showed her the globe, and we took a drink from the bottle, then another. She asked me what kind of school I went to and what my parents did for a living. She sounded like the girls at school who judged each other by what their parents made per year. I showed her my sketches, and boldly, I studied her as she looked through the pages.

Suddenly, Juliette grinned broadly and covered her face. She wore this white sundress with straps that tied at the top of her shoulders. A red stripe and a blue strip trimmed the top of the bodice and the hem of the skirt. Red, white, and blue. I wondered if she chose the dress specifically for her trip to America.

She took her hands away and pointed to the ceiling.

"They are lovers, you know, and it has been years since they have seen each other."

"Oh." I was so preoccupied with Juliette, it didn't dawn on me until then just how close Quinn and Sophie had sat together at dinner, and how they leaned in close when the other spoke.

"Sophie talks of no one but her American Quinn," Juliette said.

"Why don't they just live together?"

Juliette laughed. "Then they would not be so happy to see each other."

"They would see each other every day."

She gave me a wise smile. "Absence makes the heart grow fonder."

Juliette left me to poke around the room. She found the horn to a Victrola and bid me to help her find the rest of it. After an hour of searching, she grew bored and petulant. I grew impatient with trying to entertain her and curled up with an old anatomy book hoping she would settle down.

"I want to go to the beach," she said.

"It's nighttime," I reminded her.

"That is the best time. There is a car. We could take it."

"My aunt's car?" I asked. "I don't have a license."

She laughed. "You don't need a license, and besides, I drive in France when we go out to the country and when we go to the islands."

"Aren't the steering wheels on the opposite side?"

"Tinsley Swan has a sense of humor." Juliette grinned. "Fine, you can drive."

I rolled my eyes, though she already had me in the palm of her hand. "No one is driving. You'll just have to wait until tomorrow."

"Please?" Juliette's eyes brightened.

"Impossible." Though I was thinking of how we could make it down to the beach. Quinn's car was a decade-old Buick. I had ridden in the car when my aunt and I went to town. It seemed to have an easy temperament.

Juliette took my hand. "Our aunts will be none the wiser. They're much too busy to care if we set the house on fire."

"Fine," I said. "We'll have to be quiet."

The keys to the Buick were hanging on the peg in the kitchen. I retrieved them, and we crept out of the house and into the darkness. We closed ourselves inside the car, careful not to make too much noise. I made sure Juliette buckled herself in before I put the car in neutral without turning on the engine. We coasted around the yard and back onto the drive. Once we were at the road, I put the car in gear and drove, very slowly, down to the beach.

Before I could stop the car, Juliette flew out and ran to the water. I called after her and followed. On my way to the water, I passed a pile of fabric that gently billowed in the breeze.

Juliette's sundress.

I looked out to see her frolicking in the surf in her underwear, and laughed nervously. "Tinsley," she shouted. "Come in."

I did, bold enough to borrow my aunt's car and steal away into the night with this exotic girl, but not enough to try my hand at skinny-dipping. I kept my clothes on. We splashed in the warm darkness and ducked beneath the coursing salt water, our bodies moving together with the push and pull of the tide.

After, we lay across the trunk of the car, our backs against the window, and watched ash-colored clouds play across the violet sky sprinkled with stars. She kissed me, and the rest was a thrilling dream of fear and sensations I never imagined could exist. We returned to the house, to my room. We removed our wet clothes. Bolder now, I kissed her. She smelled and tasted of the sea. We lay on the bed; Juliette hovered above me, our bodies touching. I shivered and was embarrassed at my innocence. Juliette parted my legs and undid me in that bed, and the next morning, I was Tinsley Swan reborn. I actually began to feel like one of the Sisterhood.

Quinn recognized it when the four of us gathered for a late breakfast, and only smiled at me as we exchanged pleasantries. I had tried to act normal, but Juliette wouldn't allow it. She attended to me like a wife and flirted nonstop. It made me nervous, as I wasn't sure how the aunts would react, especially Sophie.

"You must allow my niece some space," Quinn admonished

my new lover playfully. "She is a solitary creature, who is used to keeping her desires secret."

Sophie scoffed and muttered something in French that caused Quinn to explode into laughter. Juliette covered her mouth and looked on at me worriedly.

I excused myself, fled to the library, and locked the door behind me. I expected them to come after me, but none of them did. I stared at the picture of the Golden Goddess and was sure Juliette would never want me to touch her again. I searched around the library and found the rest of the Victrola in the form of a mahogany box with gold-feathered accents. It took me an hour or so to figure out how to attach the brass horn and then the needle.

I had hoped for jazz music, but most of the discs I found were opera. I played Johanna Gadski singing Brunnhilde's battle cry and then Celestina Boninsegna singing "Bel raggio." I had gotten into the La Bohème *when Lola brought me lunch—ham sandwiches and cookies.*

"Your aunt says to eat," she said simply and left me.

I ate and sketched from the anatomy book, occasionally wondering how long they would leave me to my own devices or if they were waiting for me to come out on my own. It seemed rude to shut myself away from my aunt and her guests, but I reveled in the pleasure of doing so. My father would have never allowed it. I wondered if Juliette would want to even speak to me again, let alone take me in her arms as she did the night before. Shortly after the sphinx clock on the mantel struck five, my aunt slipped in.

"Are you finished sulking?"

"I'm sorry," I said.

"You don't have to be." She smiled. "Juliette is a spoiled, simple thing, and she will just have to understand your moods. I didn't think she would move so fast on you."

I smiled sheepishly, not sure what to say.

She sat with me before the Victrola. "I thought I had gotten rid of that god-awful thing."

I shrugged. "So no one is mad at me?"

"No, Tinsley. Juliette is upset, but she knows her place."

"Her place?" I asked.

Quinn sighed. "In a few days, you will take a high place among the Sisterhood. She knows that, and so does Sophie."

"Juliette says the others will not be happy with my initiation—"

Quinn narrowed her eyes. "She was not to discuss those things with you. I should have spoken to her myself instead of trusting Sophie."

"Please," I said. "I don't want to get her into trouble."

My aunt sighed. "Well, what's done is done. The others will come soon. You must be strong, Tinsley, or they will try to rob you of your birthright."

I nodded though I was still unsure what that birthright was. After Quinn left the library, I ventured out to find Juliette and ran into Sophie. She caught hold of my wrist sternly, and we walked out to the front porch, where she let go of me and stood staring at me.

"I'm sorry," I blurted, not sure what else to say.

She grinned, her teeth in startling contrast with her complexion. "What for?"

"Juliette, I, didn't mean to be improper—"

Sophie laughed. "You apologize, the cat who has gotten the cream, or should I say the kitten."

I looked away from her, off to the west and the last of the sun sinking low.

"I suppose Juliette has had her heart set on you. She has been mooning over you for some time now."

I looked at her, puzzled. "She's never met me."

Sophie smiled and walked to the railing. "You are the last Tinsley. Everyone has made a fuss over you since the day you were born."

I stood there for a moment, shocked at this bit of information.

"Your father turned out to be a problem," Sophie said. "He despises the Tinsleys for good reasons. They are everything his people are not, wild women with no strong man to guide them."

That certainly sounded like my father.

"Is that why the Sisters don't trust me?" I asked.

Sophie smirked. "Quinn didn't tell you that."

"No, it was Juliette."

"You're lucky to have my niece as your lover and confidante. She is a staunch devotee of the Sisterhood," she said, her tone full of pride. "I'm sure you would be as well."

She turned to me. "What Juliette shared with you, all she shared, she gives because she believes in the wisdom we protect. She is in her way preparing you for the mantle your aunt wants to appoint you."

"What mantle?" I took a tentative step forward. I wanted to understand why Juliette would show me such tenderness, a girl she hardly knew.

"That is not for me to reveal," Sophie said, her eyes glowing in the gathering darkness. "Just go to her before the poor girl worries herself to death."

She pointed toward the stables, and I ran. The lawn passed beneath me with more ease than I remembered. I had never been much of an athlete, yet there I was, sprinting effortlessly to the stable where I found Juliette in front of Abatos's stall petting his nose.

"Tinsley," she said breathlessly when she saw me.

"Hey," I said.

She ran to me and hugged me around the neck. I opened my

mouth to apologize to her, but instead, I lowered my head and planted my lips on the side of her neck. The gesture, so unfamiliar to me, turned out to be more rewarding than an apology. Juliette pulled me closer, and by the time we left the stables, darkness had long settled.

CHAPTER NINE

Juliette met us on the front lawn of Salacia. In the daylight, the unscarred portion of her face looked as smooth as a woman ten years younger. The scars on the left side of her face were a few shades lighter than her ebony skin. I wondered how she passed them off to people. It certainly looked like an animal attack. Her hair hung loose in what seemed to be endless black curls, just as they did when we were kids. She and Sandra greeted each other fondly, which sent burning-hot waves of jealousy through me.

"Hello, Tinsley," she said, her large dark eyes glinting in the sun. "I trust you didn't tell your goddess too much last night."

I narrowed my eyes at her. "She's a helpless girl," I said. "She's more afraid of the Sisterhood than anything."

Sandra edged forward out of my periphery. "She says she wants Tinsley's protection."

Juliette's eyes never left me. "What she wants is to be joined with the beast and return to the underworld."

"That's where the trouble comes in," Sandra said. "Once the gates are open, your little friend won't be able to close them behind her."

"As if she would," Juliette spat. "The Lost Goddess is not to be trusted."

I glanced up at the house. The roof was in a bad way, and the paint on the columns peeled under layers of dirt and the heat of the

Texas sun. The grass stayed trim, but there were no flowers, not like in the old days. No roaming peacocks. No smell of horses.

I turned to Sandra and took her hand, making it my point to ignore Juliette.

"I'll show you around."

We climbed the creaking front steps, and I searched for the proper keys to open the door. Sandra rang the doorbell and we heard the chime from inside.

"It's lovely," she said.

"It's a wreck," I said as the door swung open. The house was remarkably stuffy, but not stifling. I typed in the code on the pad to disarm the alarm. I opened windows and flicked on the ceiling fans.

"No AC?" Sandra asked. "Charming."

"See?" I asked.

I took my time, undraping a few of the antiques to show Sandra. We passed through to the library, and I showed her the copy of the De Sade novel where I had found Leda. She decided to share the little gem of information with Juliette.

"An actual picture?" she asked and swore in French. "And she looks exactly the same today?"

"Yes," I answered reluctantly. "Uncle Charles knew her. He said she was an innocent."

"You don't believe that, do you?" Juliette asked.

"I haven't thought about it," I said, moving to the old Victrola.

"She comes back young and beautiful each time," Juliette said, a bitterness in her voice. "This is how she draws people in, so that she may win their adoration. It is her sustenance while she plots her escape."

I thought of the people at the party and how they watched our every move together.

"So the Sisterhood has just been keeping the world from

certain doom all this time?" I asked. "I suppose they get nothing from holding a goddess ransom."

Juliette laughed bitterly. "She certainly has you."

"No one *has* me," I said. My glance strayed to Sandra, who looked doubtful. I played with the red string of Milagros around my wrist.

"Let's go to the ballroom," Juliette said.

I extended my hand and the ring of keys. "It's all yours. I'm not going in there."

"What I need to show you is in there," Juliette said. "It's just a room, Tinsley."

I turned to Sandra. "It's the room where they locked me as the beast, where I had to lock myself every seven years after that." My breathing came fast, and the lack of AC in the old house was suddenly too much.

"After I built my own house and my secret room, I swore I would never go back."

She took my hand. "I'm here with you now."

I directed my stare to Juliette, a challenge for her to contradict what I was going to say next.

"She betrayed me once. She was the bright gem, the candy my aunt Quinn used to lure me in, and she knew exactly what they were using her for."

Juliette took a step forward and snatched the keys from my hand. "I was just as innocent as you, Tinsley. I thought you had it in you to one day lead the Sisterhood. Instead you betrayed us."

"Oh really?" I asked. "And how was that?"

"You knew what would happen when you told your father about us," Juliette said. "You knew he would call the authorities. You told them the awful stories they wanted to hear, but nothing too fantastic. You didn't tell them about the beast, of course. Who would believe a story like that? Wouldn't want Daddy to think you'd lost it."

My fury faltered. How dare she turn this around on me? I was the one who had been wronged back in '83. At least Juliette had a choice about living a normal life. What choice did I have with that horrific cycle hanging over my head?

Juliette reached out and hooked a hand on my shoulder. I moved away. Sandra stepped in between us, and for a second, I hated them both.

"You ruined the Sisterhood." Juliette's face contorted with anger; the eye on the scarred side glowered fiercely. "I believe the Lost Goddess had her claws in you somehow, even then."

"I'm done," I said. "I should have known I would be caught in a bullshit barrage. I don't even know why I came here."

I stomped out into the hallway. "Keep the keys. You and the whole Sisterhood can have this damned place."

I ran out to the porch, Sandra on my heels, calling my name. She grabbed the back of my shirt and I turned to her.

"Can you believe her?" I asked. "I'm the bad guy because I stood up for myself all those years ago, because I spoke out."

"You didn't give them a chance," Sandra whispered.

"She helped them get what they wanted out of me and then she was gone," I said. "She could have come back for me when she was older. She chose them and she still is."

"You were in love with her," Sandra said. "She was your first love, and your aunt promised you the world with Juliette at your side."

"I was a stupid, stupid kid, that's what." I plopped down on the front steps.

Sandra sat next to me. She rested her head on my shoulder. "A kid with a lot of power, and as innocent as you want everyone to think. You got your revenge on the Sisterhood."

"They cursed me, and I hurt Juliette," I said.

"Is that what you're feeling, Tinsley?" Sandra asked. "Guilt?"

"No," I lied, thinking of my mother, of Quinn and Juliette.

"Finish your story," Sandra said.

I glanced back toward the house. Juliette had not joined us, and I guessed that she was digging around the ballroom, behind those massive doors in the wood-paneled chapel.

I turned back to Sandra.

"A week after Juliette and Sophie arrived, the other Sisterhood members began to show up here at Salacia."

They came from all over the world—doctors, artists, business owners, and women like Aunt Quinn, born into money and prestige. There were twenty-four members of the Sisterhood in total, and they spoke in a babble of languages, and accented English. Most of them were elderly or middle-aged, which explained why they mistrusted Juliette and me. They were introduced with titles like Sister of Ember and Sister of Fire. They called Aunt Quinn Sister of Ash, and she was the only one with that name. She was their leader.

They were courteous to me, like grown-ups are to children. There was a chill though to their niceties. Juliette had prepared me for their indifferent reception. She knew many of them already and never let me forget a name or title. There were seven different levels of the Sisterhood. Everything was in seven. They met only every seven years, on the seventh month, for seven days.

Juliette made a nice distraction. We rode down to the beach in the Buick late at night. We talked of living together in Europe when we were old enough. I began to wonder if my grown-up fantasy was not so far-fetched with Juliette in my life.

One morning before dawn, my aunt woke me and instructed me to wake Juliette and for us to dress and meet her downstairs.

"What is it?" I asked, but she was gone out the door.

I woke Juliette and told her something weird was going on.

Downstairs, the Sisterhood waited in the foyer and beyond the open door, on the porch. They began to file out of the house. I saw Aunt Quinn and went to ask her exactly what was going on. She saw me coming and put a finger to her lips. I turned to Juliette, who did the same.

We all walked across the dew-soaked front lawn and down the driveway, the older women setting the pace. We walked down the road and down the main boulevard. The sun was rising, and the townspeople were beginning to stir. They stared at us and pointed, but none of them said a word, and neither did we. I felt my cheeks burn at the scrutiny. Our solemn parade of women continued down our silent route. I looked to my aunt in an effort to try to read her, but she returned her own flat stare as if the little hike were my idea.

We came upon two lines of tall palms framing a tar-paved drive. A sign announced the Palm and Oak Cemetery, founded in 1825. An old man opened the gate and nodded. We passed through and trudged up the gravel of the main path. Cement paths divided the cemetery into smaller plots, dotted with hundreds of tiny yellow wildflowers and studded with headstones. We diverged from the main path and headed for the back of the cemetery to the mausoleums.

We passed clusters of dilapidated, broken headstones and leaning monuments stained by decades of weathering. An angel that had fallen off the top of its monument had been set up to lean casually on the stone. First, we came upon mausoleums buried when the city was leveled during the great hurricane of 1900. Only their domed peaked tops showed through the sparse grass.

Our trek ended beneath an old sprawling oak, its branches spread out in welcome. This plot was well kept, and a purple-flowered vine crawled over the east side of the mausoleum. An entablature over the door was held up by one pillar and one stone angel, her wings carved into a multitude of jagged feathers that wreathed her entire body. The plaque above the entablature read Tinsley.

Aunt Quinn walked up to the door and touched it. She turned.

"Here lies our sister Alexandrine D'Orleans, who rediscovered the mysteries of the sacred fire and brought them here to this shore. We must never forget the sacrifices she and the very first of the Sisterhood made so that we can stand here today."

"By the light of the sacred fire," Sophie shouted.

The others repeated the phrase, and I shivered recalling the dream of the burning woman and the serene look on her face. Curious about the crypt, I broke from the group and walked around to the side of the small building. On the sides, I noticed peaked windows filled with four panes of red-colored glass too rough and thick to see through. The windows were no more than a foot high and narrow, clearly for decorative purposes.

I ran my fingers over the glass. As I did, my eyes caught a shadow as if there were movement on the other side. I gasped and pulled away. I turned to see that Juliette stood behind me.

"You scared me," I said.

"What?" she asked.

I laughed at my own jumpiness. "When you passed around the building, it made a shadow on the glass."

I pointed to the small window, and on glancing down, saw a large eye staring back, surrounded by fur. The glass was suddenly smooth and seemed as thin as the film on 3-D glasses.

This time, I shrieked and stepped back, holding my arm out to keep Juliette away.

"There's some animal in there," I gasped.

"What?" Juliette asked and took a step forward. "I don't see anything, Tinsley."

I looked back at the glass. It was as opaque as the first time I noticed it.

Aunt Quinn walked around the building, a few of the others

trailing behind her. She saw my face and asked me what I had seen.

"Nothing," I said.

"She said there is an animal in there," Juliette said, and I could have died there on the spot.

Quinn studied me for a few seconds. "What sort of animal?"

I shook my head. "It was nothing, the sun, and Juliette walking behind me."

Juliette looked to my aunt. "I did not walk behind her." She crossed the distance between us and took hold of my hand. "Tell her what you saw."

"A dog," I said. "Someone has put a dog in there."

It was Quinn's turn to shake her head. The others had come to gather around the window. Some of them stared at me in what I figured was open disbelief. I made my escape around the back. Juliette followed.

"Now everyone is going to think I'm loony," I whispered to her harshly.

"No, they won't," she said. "This mausoleum is sacred to the Sisterhood. It is where Alexandrine rests and waits."

"Like she's still alive or something?" I said.

Juliette shushed me. A few of the Sisters had wandered around the back. They eyed the two of us closely, obviously scandalized. Juliette took my hand and led me to an oak tree.

"I'm not sure what exactly, but Sophie says that one day if it's necessary, one of the Sisterhood will go inside and talk to Alexandrine," she said.

I laughed. "Do you know how crazy that sounds?"

"Not as crazy as a man coming back to life after three days, or saving the earth from a flood," she said.

"It's not the same," I said. "Millions of people believe that shit. It's accepted worldwide, not just by twenty-eight broads in Galveston, Texas."

Juliette frowned. "You must not treat this as a game, Tinsley. If you appear to truly not believe, it could mean trouble for Quinn. You are the last of your line."

I gestured to the mausoleum and the gathered Sisterhood. "They don't treat me like the last of anything."

"Because you don't act like it," Juliette snapped. "This is summer vacation for you, but for them it is life."

She turned and walked away, leaving me under the oak, alone. I sulked there until Quinn came and embraced me.

"You'll know what to do when the time is right."

I sulked in the library with the door locked. I didn't care about what the Sisterhood or Juliette or Sophie would think. As far as I was concerned, they could all go to hell. Lola brought me lunch, and later, she brought me clothes for dinner. She didn't have to tell me that I was required to go. This was the sixth night, and very important according to Juliette. Sophie had taken us into town the day before so I could get new clothes. I decided to dress like the boys from school and choose light blue trousers, a pink shirt, and a bow tie, of all things. I sighed when I thought of the very grown-up dress Juliette had picked for the occasion. Even Sophie admitted that we looked gorgeous together.

I put the clothes on and slunk downstairs. Nearly all of the Sisterhood was gathered at the great table when I arrived. The dining room was in its full glory, the chandelier lit, the silver and crystal shining. I imagined the Tinsleys there instead of the strange mix of women in various periods of time—Christmas dinners, and birthdays, Easter Sundays.

Juliette sat demurely quiet as the grown-ups chatted. Her dress was a shimmery blue, and her hair was twisted back into an ebony braid. I said good evening to the women as I passed and sat next to her.

"Hi," I said.

She greeted me curtly in French. She would hardly look me in the eye.

"You're angry with me," I whispered.

"Tonight is very important," she whispered back. "Certain members of the Sisterhood will try to convince Quinn to pass her duties as Sister of Ash to another."

"Why?"

Juliette finally looked at me. "Because there is more than one of us, because we are all human beings. That's why."

"What can I do?"

"Whatever Quinn asks of you," she said.

The rest of them entered and sat. Aunt Quinn, at the head of the table, stood to make a toast. She wore a flowing white dress that fell off her shoulders. Her hair she had twisted and pulled up into a reddish-gold crown around her head. Next to her sat Sophie dressed in black. She regarded me from the far side of the large room with tense, dark eyes.

"Tonight," Quinn said. "I formally welcome my progeny, Sister of Flame, Tinsley Swan. Unlike young Juliette, I initiated her myself, and I know this has caused a lot of confusion—"

A middle-aged woman in a full tuxedo cleared her throat loudly and spoke. "It is not confusion we feel, but dismay that you would shirk tradition and show favor to your blood."

Quinn tilted her head and gave a cold smile. "My dear Sister of Ember, has my bloodline always kept the Sisterhood afloat, sacrificed to keep its wisdom safe?"

Another woman spoke. She was elderly, her hair like wispy cobwebs escaped from a teal-colored turban she wore on her head with a large jewel in the middle of her forehead.

"And is not this child the last of your line?" she asked. "Is it not true that she has known nothing of the Sisterhood until a few days ago when you gave her the rites?"

A wave of disapproving murmurs passed through the dining room.

Juliette's hand covered mine, and I noticed that I had been trembling. I looked to her and she pulled her lips into a flat line.

At that moment, I would have done anything for her. I glanced back at Quinn.

"So we have factions now?" she was asking.

"Factions you started," someone shouted.

Sophie stood with Quinn. "Who are you to argue with the Sister of Ash, a descendant of Alexandrine herself?"

My aunt's gaze fell on me, then she quickly turned away. She went to the dining room doors and slid them closed as she spoke to the serving crew outside. She calmly walked to the other side of the room and closed the other doors. On her way back to her spot at the table, she retrieved a wooden box. She brought it back to the table and handed it to me.

"Open it," she whispered. "I pray you know what to do."

With trembling fingers, I opened the box. The face that stared up at me from a bed of red silk startled me. It was the horned face from the ballroom. I nearly backed away from the table, until I remembered that it was only a mask. I lifted it from the box. A collective gasp rushed through the room. I turned the mask over in my hands, ran my fingers over the stiff hairs that lined the inside. The feel of it disgusted me.

"Tinsley, you must," Quinn said, having sensed my hesitation.

I put the mask in front of my face and held it there, as there was no strap or ribbon to hold it in place. Through the eyeholes, my eyes passed over the women gathered in the room staring at me, and I nearly laughed. They looked as terrified as I felt that night, drunk on Quinn's wine.

The bristly hairs moved against my skin, a sickening ripple. I felt faint, nauseous, but also energized, as if I wanted to run howling from the room at full tilt. A ripple of blackness passed over my vision, and I was moving right over the table. I saw the astonished faces of the women, and I could vaguely hear the clatter of china and silver.

Then my hands were touching the chandelier. One of my

shoes floated down and crashed onto someone's place setting.
I noticed Juliette grinning as she looked up at me. I wanted to
be with her, and suddenly was there next to her, my hands in her
hair.

Juliette showed no fear. She touched my—no—the horned
one's face as two tears escaped her eyes. She whispered my name,
a slight grin on her face.

The black wave returned like a tide, and I was back in my
chair. The dining room table was a mess, the tablecloth twisted,
the settings turned over or broken, candles leaking wax on the
fine dark wood. The women were on their feet and looking at me
as dots and tiny shards of white light danced over their faces.

I tilted my head up, saw the chandelier swaying back and
forth.

"The beast has chosen its vessel," my aunt announced
triumphantly.

No one argued with her.

I decided to speak up. "I know what you all think of me," I
said. "Most of it is true. My father would not approve of this, and
I realize now that he was instrumental in keeping me from my
mother's family."

I looked to Quinn and saw that her eyes watered as if she
would cry, Sophie touched her shoulder and the two held hands,
the most intimate gesture I had seen between them so far.

"That doesn't mean I cannot learn what it means to be part
of the Sisterhood, that I cannot keep your secret wisdom. I like it
here at Salacia, and I care for Aunt Quinn."

Out of the corner of my eye, I could feel Juliette beaming at
me. I took my seat and felt her arms around me as the women in
the room weakly applauded my words. At the head of the table,
Aunt Quinn bowed her head to me.

Suddenly, a pain rippled through my back; the muscles there
seemed to be at war. I fell forward onto my place setting, shaking
so hard my teeth chattered. The bones in my feet felt as if they had

been shattered. I screamed as the edges of my sight darkened. I heard fabric tear, watched black claws curl from the ends of my fingertips. I smelled blood.

I fell from the table to the floor, saw Aunt Quinn dragging Juliette away as she reached out her hands to me, red blood cloaked the left side of her face, and still she called my name. One of her arms glowed with red rivulets of blood. The darkness took over and swallowed me whole.

Chapter Ten

S andra held tight to my hand as we sat on the porch in silence. A mild breeze floated our way, and I could smell the Gulf on it.

"I saw Juliette the next day, when the other Sisters burned the seven-sided star into our chests," I said. "She wanted to complete her initiation. She wanted to dance before the sacred fire. Her eyes were hazy, and she was bandaged. That night, I became the beast, and I woke a week later, chained in that awful chapel."

I jerked my head toward the house and caught a glimpse of Juliette standing in the doorway. I turned to see her fully and saw the wooden box tucked under arm.

"That was an unfortunate accident. An anomaly, I was told," Juliette said.

"Why did you stay?" I asked her.

She shook her head and stepped out into the daylight. "It was my duty because it was in my blood, even if that blood was spilled. I had to grow up fast, Tinsley. I couldn't be a teenager in love."

She extended her arms, the box cradled on her forearms and palms. "Quinn hoped that one day you would be ready to join the Sisterhood. She didn't know that the Lost Goddess was one step ahead of us."

I stood, but I did not go near the box. "I'm ready to go," I told Sandra.

"Tinsley," she whispered. "You can't walk away."

"I will," I said.

Juliette used one hand to flip open the lid of the box. It clattered to the floor of the porch, causing both Sandra and me to jump. I saw the contents on a bed of velvet and turned my face away.

"This is your legacy," Juliette told me.

"Get it the fuck away from me." I stumbled backward off the porch.

Sandra stepped forward. A curious expression on her face. She reached in, removed the old horned mask with one hand and that horrible gold handled crop with the other.

"No," I shouted as if she were handling uranium. "Put that down."

I remembered how disgusting the lining of it felt on my face, those bristling hairs, and how they had moved against my skin. The thought of that hideous thing touching my lovely Sandra alarmed me to no end.

She held the objects with a familiarity that was equally startling. She held on to the crop's handle loosely, and the mask she balanced on the fingertips of her opposite hand. Slowly, she raised it to her face. Unafraid. She looked at me through the eyeholes, and I knew.

I staggered backward, my heart seizing in this cold revelation.

"You're one of them," I said. "You're one of the Sisterhood."

Sandra returned the mask to the box, the crop as well. "Tinsley," she said. Her voice was soft, like those mornings when we woke together. She had known everything, the entire time. She had known to come into the ladies' room and exactly what she would find.

"You shouldn't blame her," Juliette said. "She only wanted to reach out to you."

I ignored her. My eyes were glued on Sandra. "How could you do this to me?"

"Tinsley," she said calmly. "I'm sorry."

"You lied," I said.

She stepped forward, her eyes wide and watery. "The part where I cared for you was no lie. What you felt for me, I felt it right back."

My heart shuddered, and my ribs began to convulse. The beast. I fell into the grass on my hand and knees, fighting the change.

"Stay back," I said, my voice now a growl.

Juliette and Sandra exchanged glances but made no move to help. As if I would want either of them near me. I roared at them. My entire body froze in one huge spasm, as if my entire self threatened to course out of me. My hands sprouted hair and my fingers extended into curved black claws, tearing away the grass to the black soil beneath. Sandra's string of Milagros snapped and the charms fell into the grass. Whatever miracles I thought she had brought me were all deceits. I heard my shirt rip.

Behind me came the sound of an engine and tires on the loose gravel. I whipped my head around to see a large burgundy-colored van charging toward the house. It halted and the rocks under the tires popped in different directions. The side door slid open. Pearl, the girl from Little Foxes, stuck her head out.

"Tinsley," she called. "Come on."

I looked back to the front door of Salacia. Juliette had a hand in front of Sandra, who took a tentative step forward. She called my name as well.

Pearl spoke again. "We've come to get you."

I lurched to my feet, limped toward the van, and climbed inside. Pearl slid the door closed, shutting out the sunlight.

"Shit," she said, kneeling next to me.

I saw Claudio's massive head in the driver's seat. "I didn't know you were so popular with the ladies."

I moved to sit up, but another form in the darkened interior of the van placed a hand on my chest. A light glowed beneath her hand, and I was calm.

"Leda," I said.

"Poor Tinsley," she whispered. She cradled my head in her lap.

"Sandra," I said and realized I was back to my normal human woman's body. "She's one of the Sisterhood. All this time."

"Just chill," she said and I knew she was smiling.

I sighed. "I heard your voice that night in the pyre."

"It's much different this time around," Leda said. "I felt it the moment I woke. I knew you were close by, waiting."

Lulled by her voice and the swaying of the van, I closed my eyes.

The day after the dinner party, I did not wake until well past noon. My first thought was of Juliette. She was not there in the room with me, so I went to the room previously designated for her, to find it empty. I didn't bother to change out of my pajamas. I searched the house and only found those strange women, the Sisterhood, staring at me wordlessly. I went to the library to find it empty as well. I began to call out frantically for Juliette. I felt feverishly hot and nauseous.

I staggered out to the yard. A crew of men labored to stack tall lengths of wood in a cone shape. I went farther out and found Quinn at the stables trotting the Walker, Nonios, in a tight circle. She smiled when she saw me and dismounted. She guided me away from the horses, and I was grateful, as their smell was maddeningly strong.

"What happened last night, and that other night in the ballroom?" I asked.

"Your birthright," Quinn said. "The transformation is one of the greatest secrets of the Sisterhood."

"Transformation into what? That mask thing?"

"We all make great sacrifices," she said. "Don't you think I would love to have a child of my own?" She reached out and touched my face longingly.

"Where is Juliette?"

"She's at a hotel in town," Quinn said. "Resting for tonight, as you should be."

"A hotel?" I asked. "Why?"

Quinn looked sympathetic. "The poor thing was overwhelmed last night at what she saw. There are still things that are secret to her, you know."

I felt of wave of nausea pass through me, and I promptly threw up in the grass. Quinn rubbed my back and spoke softly. I wanted Juliette there instead.

"Can't she come back?" I asked.

"You'll see her tonight," Quinn told me as she led me back to the house. She chuckled. "She's got her claws deep, hasn't she?"

At the word claws a new wave of nausea passed through me. I remembered black claws at the ends of my fingers, the agonizing pain, and how it was soothed when they pierced flesh and drew blood.

I retched again. This time I fought Quinn's comforting touch. When I was done, I straightened as best I could. She stood over me in the light of the high Texas sun, her red hair like stylized flame.

"You've made me into a monster," I sobbed. "I hurt Juliette."

Quinn took a step forward and I moved away. "Tinsley, the silly girl will be fine. Her scars are a blessing."

"Scars?" I asked.

Quinn sighed. "Every seven years the stars of this world and the underworld align the exact same way. The barriers in between weaken and we light the sacred fire to keep this world safe. Every seven years you will turn, and that is how you will stay for seven days and seven nights. I will keep you safe—"

"You put that mask on me and made me into this thing?"

"The beast," Quinn said. "The familiar to the Lost Goddess. We do all of this to protect the gateway between the worlds."

"I didn't want this," I said, edging away when she moved forward.

"You've already agreed, Tinsley, that night when you put on the mask."

"I didn't put on shit," I shouted. "You tricked me."

She grabbed my arm. "You agreed because deep down, you know that this is your legacy."

"Let go of me," I stammered, nearly in tears. "I'm going back to Houston, and I'm going to tell my father about those horrid women and what you did to me."

Quinn slapped me. I held my stinging cheek, shocked.

"The world of men is not your sanctuary." She pointed at the house. "These women would have lost their wealth generations ago. They certainly wouldn't have become venerated in their fields. Every seven years, we gather to bathe in the glow of the sacred fire, and every seventy years, the Lost Goddess imbues us with her light."

Quinn shoved me away roughly. I tripped over my own feet and fell to the grass. "Go to your father if you feel he will ever pass on any type of enlightenment to his pitiful girl child."

I entered the house and headed for the steps, but several of the Sisterhood blocked my way. One of them held a leather strap, the other a red sack. I backed away, toward the door. Casting a glance over my shoulder, I saw that even more of them blocked the way. Weakened by fear and exhaustion, my body collapsed.

They surged forward as one and caught hold of me. They tore away my pajama top.

"Let go of me," I shouted at them.

Aunt Quinn stepped forward. Sunlight streamed in through the open door behind her, illuminating the red in her hair, transforming it into a halo of fire.

"You are the familiar now, Tinsley, and soon you will understand everything."

One of the Sisterhood handed her a wooden box. Quinn opened it to reveal a small pile of smoldering ashes, their glow strong in the light of day.

"Every year, we call upon the Sacred Fire," Quinn said. "These are some of the ashes from the previous pyre."

I found myself transfixed by the contents of the box and quickly forgot my struggle with the Sisterhood. One of them stepped next to Quinn, holding what looked to be a cattle brand with a silver medal etched with a seven-sided star symbol, like the one tattooed on my aunt's chest.

Sophie appeared with a small torch. She held it while the other woman touched the brand into the flame. The realization of what they were doing crept into my brain, and I began to struggle again.

After a minute, the brand was dipped into the box and covered with the glowing embers. Sophie took hold of it and pressed the hot metal above my barely budded breast. I screamed at the pain that radiated through the layers of my skin and down to the muscle. Sophie pulled the brand away. I could smell burning skin.

My knees buckled and I fell fast. They caught me and forced the bag over my head. My breath caught in my lungs, and I had to force myself to breathe. When I did, I smelled a sickening sweetness. Under the darkness of the hood, swirling colors sparked in front of my eyes.

When I heard the strain of metal hinges, I knew we were going into the ballroom.

I felt them all immediately, their eyes upon me. They sat me on one of the cushioned wooden stools. They took my shoes. I wondered if Juliette was there and called out her name weakly. Someone I identified as Sophie told me to hush. I smelled dusky smoke through the hood, and it mingled with the sweetness.

I felt my body relax, though my mind continued to go a million miles a minute. I saw stars, deep space like the artistic renderings of nebulae I was fond of looking at in my school's library. I felt as if I simultaneously spun helplessly out in the universe while still being there in the ballroom, my butt on a cushion, my feet on the warm wooden floor.

Someone began to speak, a sort of prayer I half heard as the winds of creation blew a cold wind about my head.

"She who is the fire. She who is destruction. She who hunts the night with the great beast."

A supernova exploded in slow motion, and I felt my face burn as if I had been out in the sun too long. I must have fallen over, because I felt strong hands sit me back up onto the stool.

"She who is the Phoenix. The reborn."

A bright light flashed behind my eyes, and I saw through unfocused eyes my mother. I heard her singing to me in the distance. I felt her kiss on my face as well as streams of tears.

"She brought us the great wisdom, and we made her our captive."

I saw the great fire from my dream and the woman inside. She regarded me with violet eyes. She spoke in a whispery rush, and at first, I couldn't understand what she said.

"Give me what is mine, foolish girl, and I will spare you my vengeance."

Light, suddenly, and hands on my face. Aunt Quinn stood before me in her blood-red kimono. Behind her roared a great fire. I expected to see a woman among the flames. Instead, I saw the silhouettes of the other sisters, some in orange and black, others in yellow and brown.

I blinked. We were out in the yard, and the woodpile I saw being stacked earlier was ablaze. Someone began to pound a drum, and someone started to play a high-pitched flute.

I saw Juliette clothed in nothing but strategically placed gauzy scraps of fabric. Her arm and the side of her face were bandaged. She began to dance, a slow sway. She untied one of the swaths and tossed it aside. The primitive music picked up, and she dashed to one side of the fire and pirouetted on one foot before falling to the ground, only to gracefully rise again. She removed another piece, revealing her breasts. It was only then that I noticed my own nakedness.

Juliette arched her back and danced in a tight circle; she shed another piece. This continued until seven swaths had fallen to the ground and she was completely naked. By then the music had reached a wild rhythm.

A dozen or so sisters stood on either side of her. She danced away from them, but they crowded her, shielding her from my sight. In the light of the fire, I saw them all dance a slow, choreographed struggle that disturbed me.

The fire burned brighter and higher, seeming to take on a life of its own. Once it reached a certain height, it bent over like a sapling too weak to hold its own weight.

"She comes," Quinn said and placed the mask on my face.

A sudden wind whipped the flames of the fire into a wild frenzy. It seemed to stretch miles into the star-filled sky and burn as bright as the sun. On the ground, sparks lit the grass as if thousands of lightning bugs had lit amongst the blades. I shivered at the sight.

The beast took over my body in just a few bone-crunching, muscle-tearing minutes of agony that caused me to feel nauseous. My first full transformation. I writhed in the grass like a slug doused with salt.

Quinn backed away, her eyes on me, the crop and whip in her hands.

The strange wind picked up. Claimed by agony, I watched the Sisters crouch low as tendrils of fire whipped over their heads.

Then the beast was up. The pain was gone. Quinn stepped in front of the beast, brandishing her crop and flail. They frightened me on a truly primal level. The beast hated and feared them at once. It lowered itself to the grass and growled.

The sparks in the grass rose into the air. They lit the face of my aunt, Quinn Tinsley, Sister of Ash, tamer of the beast. She circled slowly, crouched low, her steps slow and deliberate.

The beast leapt at her. Quinn lashed out and dodged with the grace of a bullfighter. The other members backed away, their frightened faces blurred in the firelight. Quinn lunged again; this time, her weapons made contact. They burned the beast. She struck the beast again, and things went black.

I woke seven days later in the chapel. Quinn stood over me in her red kimono. Neither of us said a word as she stooped and draped me in a very large towel and led me out of the chapel. The daylight stung my eyes.

Quinn put me in a tub of warm water and began to wash my back. I cried a little more as flashes of memories from the past week flickered through my brain. I remembered the voice that had spoken to me through the fire and shivered.

Quinn moved to look at my face. She smiled wanly.

"Why do we hold her captive?" I asked. "Why did we have to take what is hers?"

Quinn bit her lip worriedly. "She spoke to you."

"Who is she?"

"A goddess, a willful spirit who will do what she can to take the beast from you," Aunt Quinn explained. "She cannot hurt you."

She helped me out of the tub, as docile as a lamb. She dried me, dressed me, and put me to bed. I sank into the soft mattress.

"What have you done to me?" I said.

"You must stop this." She leaned over me. "What is done is done. The memory of it will fade, and one day you will be able to see Juliette again."

The thought of her did little to comfort me. "Can you undo this?"

Quinn closed her eyes and sighed. "No, Tinsley."

"Will this happen to me forever?" I asked and tried to get out of bed. She held me there.

"Every seven years when we burn the great pyre, you will transform. It will last for seven days," Quinn said. "As the years go by, this will get better for you, and we will always be here to help you."

I gave up my fight and sobbed. "What if you don't light the fire?"

"We must in order to keep this world safe."

"I didn't get to say good-bye to Juliette. It's not fair to rip us apart like this."

Quinn smiled. "Look at you, Tinsley. You've changed so much in a short time, and now you carry within you a great power."

"It doesn't belong to me."

Quinn leaned over and kissed my cheek. "Sleep. You need rest now."

I slept again, but woke in the night thirsty. I drank from the bathroom sink and then undressed to bathe. I happened to look at my backside in the mirror and saw the tattoo. At once, I saw a flash of frightened faces, the whites of the eyes of the horses as they reared in terror, and I heard the fire-voice demanding what was hers.

I looked at my reflection. "You should have taken it and left me alone."

In the quiet of the night, I bathed and dressed. I found my knapsack that I used to pack my summer reading. Those books seemed so ridiculous to me then, trifles. I put an extra shirt, underpants, my toothbrush, and Tylenol for my pains in that backpack, then went down to the library. From under the desk lamp, I removed the cover of Justine and replaced it with one from a copy of Leaves of Grass.

Downstairs, I stole the keys to the Buick. As I had with Juliette, I coasted out of the drive and started the engine when I was far enough out of hearing range.

I was only a child, running home to my mother and father. In the months that followed, what I told my parents ripped my family apart. My mother killed herself one night that December, just a few days before Christmas.

Quinn came to her funeral, though she had fled the country with several American members of the Sisterhood. She looked as if she had aged twenty years, and her clothes billowed around her. When one of my father's brothers asked her to leave, she caused a scene. When she saw me watching, she shouted, "What have you done, Tinsley? What will you take from me next?"

She left the country before the trial, abandoned Salacia. For years after, I imagined her somewhere with Sophie and Juliette. As for my first lover, I never spoke of her to my father or the therapists he sent me to. It was my way of protecting her, my way of apologizing for taking away her beloved Sisterhood.

I forgot about Juliette, and I forgot about the goddess in flames demanding what was hers. I forgot the horses mangled in their stalls. I forgot about changing into a beast. I forgot that night when Juliette danced naked before a pyre of flames.

Every now and then, I would slide those postcards from that book so deceptively covered. The beast came to me every seven years. I went to Salacia and shut myself in the house. Except for work, I kept to myself. In my twenties, there was the occasional woman, but I never let her into my life. In my thirties, I fully embraced my solitude. I had my career, my postcards. I eventually built my secret room in my fortress on Valentine Street, and for good measure, I built one around my heart.

CHAPTER ELEVEN

They took me to a house in an old but well-kept neighborhood of Houston. Claudio carried me into a small stucco-covered house. Inside, several young women lounged around in their summer clothes, listening to obnoxious pop music. They didn't seem to notice my arrival until Leda stepped in behind us.

"Everyone. Get the fuck out of here," she said.

A chorus of disagreement bubbled forth from the young women as they gathered their handbags and smartphones to leave. Claudio dumped me on a vacated couch and lumbered out of the house with the others.

Leda didn't say a word. She only stood staring at me beneath her heavy-lidded eyes. She wore her hair in curls, but they were raven's-wing black.

I managed to sit up a bit. My blouse had not been torn too badly in the transformation. I gathered it around me protectively.

"What happened back there?"

"It's the beast's nature to choose my side in this. They no longer need the beast to help them seek me out. They were going to induce the transformation and lock you away."

My heart clenched, and tears threatened my eyes as I thought of Sandra, the kindness and tenderness she had shown me.

"How do you know this?" I asked.

Leda stood. "I've played this game many times before,

across the ages." She walked barefoot across the wooden floor to a portable bar stocked with various liquors.

"Sandra pretended to care for me. She was one of the Sisterhood the whole time," I explained. "I actually thought…"

Leda brought me a very large martini and placed it in my shaking hands. She sat next to me on the sofa and sipped from a short snifter.

"The beast is the weak point in this game," she said. "Whoever controls the beast controls the game. Even now, with you so close, I cannot take it."

I snorted. "I would give it to you." I paused and took a swig of martini, eyeing her around the rim of the glass. "They say if you ever had the beast it would mean the end of the world."

She laughed bitterly. "The end of their world. They would no longer have my power at their disposal, and I would go to the underworld, out of their reach.

"I have more than suffered for whatever transgressions I committed," Leda said decidedly. "I deserve to return from where I came, to go back to eternity."

Stunned, I drained my glass. I would have to eat soon or else be sick.

"Would that mean danger to this world?"

"The physical world has pleased me greatly over the centuries. I feel like I'm one of the last patrons of humankind, and I would never see harm come to it. Even if it meant my sacrifice." She took my hand. "Come and I will show you."

We went down a short hallway to the back of the house to a darkened room with a bed and a stand with a mirror on top. I heard a drawer open, and Leda placed a bundle of soft fabric in my hands. Another shirt. I rid myself of the torn one and put the new one on.

Leda opened a door that led to a deck built around a towering pecan tree. There were a few chairs with cushions strewn about, and two short glass tables. A high wooden fence surrounded the area.

Leda kneeled in front of a terra-cotta chiminea and directed me to do the same. With a fireplace lighter, she lit the contents of the open belly. As the flame began to grow, I saw that her tinder was a ball of dried flowering plants and herbs on a pile of sticks. There was something holistically primal about the fire. I smelled sage as a thin column of smoke rose from the vent on top.

Leda stared into the flame. The glow from the fire seemed to infuse her skin. She turned to me, and I saw that a light did radiate beneath her skin, a flickering orange light as if her blood were on fire.

After a moment, she looked back into the chiminea.

I did the same. The edges of the world blurred as if I were moving in a fast car, and I found that the world around us had changed. The little terra-cotta fireplace was a great, roaring head of stone, and tongues of flame issued from its fanged mouth.

I looked back to Leda, and in her place saw walls made of stones and a doorway of large blocks in a primitive post and lintel. Night waited beyond, and more stars than I have ever seen in the sky. I heard a voice and turned to see a procession of brown-skinned people. The women among the group were young and wore white linen robes that left little to the imagination. The men were older and shaved bald. One of them wore a tall crown of hammered gold. They were adorned with various gold cuffs and jeweled collars. They carried bowls of fruit, and grain, and raw meat.

Leda walked out to greet them. Her robe was dyed black but was sheer enough to reveal the silhouette of her breasts and the press of her nipples. The robe opened to reveal a golden girdle. She carried a flail in one hand, a crook in the other.

In the polished reflection, I saw myself as the beast with the face of a lioness with a crown of seven horns, the body and tail of a dragon, and four legs, the back ones stouter and longer than the front, which had almost ape-like digits but clawed.

I crouched low next to Leda. The smell of incense prickled my nostrils. More interesting to me were the smells of the people in the procession. They began to file forward past the older man and shuffle toward the table, on which they each placed a gift of fruit, meat, golden beads, or blue stones. They kept their eyes downcast except to steal second glances, as if looking directly at Leda was forbidden.

The old man gestured to the table and spoke his ancient language in a reverent tone.

Leda spoke back in the lilting tongue. The old man closed his eyes serenely and nodded in a low bow. As Leda continued to speak, her tone grew grave, her voice echoed throughout the stone room.

The fire blazed brighter as she spoke, stirred by a sudden chilly breeze. The white robes of the procession billowed as they all fell to their knees and pressed their foreheads to the floor. The old priest lowered himself to the floor. He was pleading now, his voice shaking.

All the while, I paced and prowled a tight space near Leda, tethered to her side by an unseen chain, excited by her anger. I shivered and shook. The chain snapped and I was upon the old priest, my black claws tangled in his white robe, tearing his skin and staining it red with his blood.

I startled to present day and saw that the fire in the chiminea was nothing but dying cinders. Leda was still next to me, watching. I felt at once thrilled and sickened by what I had seen.

"That is what we were, the beast and I, my familiar. People worshipped and feared me. I gave and I took at my own whim." She closed her eyes, the memory sweet to her.

"Such power, Tinsley, and it was taken from me."

I shook my head. "That's not what I wanted."

She touched my hand. "I know."

"We should get out of here," I told her. "Anywhere in the world you want to go. I'll take you there."

She smiled. "There is something I must do here first."

"What?" I asked.

She looked back into the fire. "Tomorrow is the pride parade."

"The pride parade?" I stood.

Leda extended her hand and looked up at me. "I have a plan. Something that will help us in our flight."

I helped her to her feet and she snuggled close. "Would you be mine tonight, Tinsley?"

"What?" I asked, not sure if I wanted to bring myself to comprehend what she was asking of me. My stomach growled, and I thanked the heavens that other parts of me couldn't express their desires.

She laughed. "I could be yours. Certainly."

I moved away from her. "The transformation takes a lot out of me. I need to rest."

She followed. "I know just the place to take you."

We walked to a Thai place a few blocks away in a little storefront. The place was even smaller than the outside suggested, and misty with food and smoke. A few patrons ate or puffed from hookah pipes. I wondered if the owners knew about the city ordinance against smoking. The staff seemed to know her, and they began to bring out food right away, deep-fried bread with a spicy chicken mixture on top, grilled strips of beef in a spicy glaze, and a soup of shrimp in a coconut milk broth. Even though I had never tried Thai food before, I was ravenous. I ate everything while she smoked from a hookah pipe and drank glass after glass of rice whiskey straight.

"Don't you have to eat?" I asked as I scarfed down a noodle stir-fry.

"No," she said. "It doesn't bring me any pleasure."

"Is that how you get by?" I asked. "Pleasure?"

She took a pull of smoke from her pipe and blew it away. She lifted her eyes and gestured with her chin behind me. I turned to see Juliette of all people, and Sandra two steps behind her. I turned around to face Leda again. She sat smoking calmly.

They came to our table dragging two chairs with them. I tried to stare daggers through Sandra as she sat.

"We all need to talk," Juliette said.

"Me first," Sandra said. She looked to me. "Tinsley, I never meant to hurt you. I have a distant aunt who found me in eighty-six. She's a member of the Sisterhood. My family goes back pretty far."

"When were you going to tell me?" I asked.

Juliette opened her mouth to speak, but Sandra raised a hand to silence her. "Think about it. None of the sisters who ever carried the beast turned away from their duties, none of them ever heard the Lost Goddess speak to them from the fire, and none of them ever found pictures of her."

"She set it all up," Juliette growled, pointing her finger at Leda who, in reply, let out a short stream of fragrant smoke. "She's had you under some kind of glamour all these years."

She reached into her jacket and removed my postcards, the two of Leda. She slapped them unceremoniously on the table. Leda raised her eyebrows as her gaze wavered between her likeness in black and white, in repose and in armor.

"You broke into my house."

"You're not seeing," Sandra pleaded and placed a hand over the postcards. "She put her spell on you before you were even properly initiated."

"How would she do that?" I asked. "She wasn't around."

Sandra glared at Leda, and then at me, her eyes softening. "Just get up and come with me. I'll take you home. Tomorrow night, you'll change, and when it's over, I'll be waiting for you, just as we planned."

Her words refreshed the realization that she had lied to me, that she had infiltrated my job, cozened and cajoled her way into my bed with her promises.

"Are you even a real designer?" I asked.

She sighed. "Honey, I'm more talented than all those hacks at OddDuck."

I nearly smiled.

A waitress approached with a tray with a green clay tea service and four glasses. She carefully set it down. Juliette reached for the steaming teapot, and I knew something was wrong before her fingers could grasp the handle.

Leda knew as well. She hissed and floated away from the table, her violet irises bleeding into the whites of her eyes. She bowled over another small table, some chairs, and a passing elderly server.

Juliette stood and, with a flick of her wrist, tossed the contents of the pot toward Leda. Instead of tea, orange and red embers burned an arc across the space between Juliette and Leda.

I was up as well, but not for long. The change came over me, and I collapsed to the floor, on my back, writhing in pain. I heard Leda scream, and I rolled over and pulled myself forward, the black claws gouging ruts into the linoleum.

I crawled toward Leda and looked up to see her face marred by burning holes. Orange patches glowed behind the melted skin. At her right shoulder, the flesh fell away in clumps of cinders and crumbled into ash as they hit the floor. Her eyes met mine as another scream escaped her glowing throat.

I jumped to my feet and answered her anguish with a roar that seemed to shake the entire building. I sailed in front of Leda as Juliette jumped on top of the table, that horrible crop raised above her head, the flail in the other. I swiped at her, saw my hairy, clawed hand impact her chest, saw her face change from determination to fear.

She flew backward and crashed into the fat man's mini-buffet. His young companion screamed as the table fell over sending food, drink, and eating utensils raining to the floor. Sandra watched the scene calmly. She looked to me and said my name slowly and sternly as if she were talking to a spooked horse. She took a tentative step forward. I shouted for her to stay back, but of course, it came out in the form of another soul-shaking roar.

I felt an arm snake around my neck, and a hand tangled in the fur around my back.

"Get me out of here, Tinsley," Leda said.

I leapt forward on all fours, my claws scrambling through the restaurant debris on the floor. Bits of embers and ash flew across my field of vision, and I knew they came from Leda, that she was hurt. Juliette rose, brandishing her weapons. I skirted around her and jumped on a counter, knocking over a cash register and its screen.

Juliette came at me in a full run, Sandra close behind.

I sank down on my haunches and jumped at the window of the storefront, claws first. The plate glass shattered to bits in a smoky blue explosion. I landed on my feet on the sidewalk. I took only a second to pause to make sure Leda still held on, and then I was off again.

I ran away, right into the street where cars darted to avoid hitting me. I leapt over a full-sized pickup and landed, claws scrambling for purchase in its plastic-lined bed. The brakes protested as the startled driver stopped. The force of the sudden stop slammed me into the back windshield. Leda fell into the truck bed on her side. I leaned over her, certain she was dead, that the Sisterhood had succeeded in burning her.

I heard a gasp and looked up to see the owner of the truck staring. A low growl rumbled from my throat, and the man fled.

Leda stirred. She grabbed two tufts of my hair and lifted herself to her feet. Her skin still glowed where the embers had touched her, but otherwise she seemed to have regenerated. She stumbled a bit, and I leaned into her so she could stand.

Sirens reported in the distance. Leda climbed on my back again. I leapt out of the truck and onto the sidewalk. I scaled the fence of a large cemetery, sprinted across the grounds, and over the opposite fence. Careful of the burden on my back, I moved in the cover of dark and several underpasses of busy streets built high above Buffalo Bayou.

Despite the presence of the beast that dominated my mind, I was headed home. I stopped at an oak-shaded intersection where a rickety church presided over a group of row houses, dilapidated and abandoned except for the most lost members of society. I stopped and Leda slid off my back. The skin at her face and arm continued to glow, though not as bright as before. Her eyes were nearly closed from exhaustion.

I could not take her home. The Sisterhood was more than likely watching for my return. I squatted next to Leda and waited for her to give me some kind of direction. She said nothing and began to doze against the trunk of the oak. I heard voices, men talking loud and brash as they made their way around the block. Once again, I lifted Leda and moved toward the row houses. A warm breeze carried a dozen scents my way—grass, decay, scat, rotting wood, and sewage.

I climbed the cinderblock steps that led to the back porch of one of the houses where the screen door had fallen away. I peered into the shadowy interior of the kitchen. Inside, grime and filth layered the broken vinyl on the floor. I smelled the moist musk of small animals beneath the rotting floorboards and years-old grease. I backed away when I heard voices coming from somewhere inside the house. A resounding creaking noise was followed by the snapping of splintering wood as two of the floorboards gave. My foot crashed through one of the worn wooden boards that barely held the porch together.

Leda fell along with me, and I scrambled to free myself from the hole. Once I was free, I looked for Leda, only to find that she was gone. The voices in the house began to chatter excitedly. Their high-pitched tones told me they were children.

Quickly, I made my way into the house, through the kitchen, and into the small living room. There I saw Leda surrounded by a group of children. They were admiring her glowing skin under the light of candles. One of them pointed the beam of a flashlight into my eyes.

"Transmorphation," they exclaimed in unison.

The Sun Monster kids. I scrambled away from them and became tangled in a gutted wall of broken wood and wires. They moved in as I extricated myself. The boy Bobby stood among them. He reached out with an extended finger to touch me.

"Does it hurt?" he asked.

I roared at him. The children startled but none of them moved. Ignorant children, so blinded by a make-believe world created by a conglomerate of entertainment companies eager to sell them useless myth that they didn't realize what danger they were in.

"It's okay," Leda said and then spoke to the children. "You're making my friend nervous."

They all gathered around her once again, squatting on milk crates.

"Are you a Fire Pixie?" one of them asked.

"Yes," she said and allowed them to touch her arm and face. The glow slowly vanished, to the children's disappointment. Leda seemed to gain her strength back. She sat among them and looked through their collectable cards.

I squatted in the darkest corner. Bobby tiptoed in and tried to give me a Snickers and a can of Pepsi as if this were some ridiculous movie about another boy adventurer. I growled evenly.

They had drawn the Sun Monster symbols all over the walls, as well as crude drawings of the most popular of the creatures. If I had been in a better humor, I would have laughed. Were we all not children in the dark drawing graffiti and following even more ridiculous myths?

I changed back into my own skin and crossed my arms over my chest.

"Professor Swiggleslock," Bobby said in amazement.

He took off his oversized T-shirt and gave it to me to cover myself, and I thanked him.

"That Dark Agent figured out I was spying on her," he said. "She was pissed."

"Did she scare you?" I asked and found my voice hoarse and scratchy.

"She told me to look out for you." He smiled. "She gave me twenty dollars."

I rolled my eyes. "All of you should go home," I told them. "It's late."

They exchanged glances as if they had to decide if I could tell them what to do. They looked to Leda as if she held more authority.

"We can play tomorrow," Bobby finally said, and they began to drift off. I reached out and grabbed his arm when he moved to follow them.

"If you ever see the Dark Agent lady again, tell her that was a dirty trick she played."

He grinned, pleased to be involved in this bit of intrigue. He left behind the soda and candy, and I felt so depleted that I devoured them as soon as he left. Leda watched me while she removed her cell from her pocket and called Claudio. She told him where we were.

"Make sure you're not followed. Alexandrine's cult is everywhere."

"They've been following us," I said once she ended the call.

"For some time," Leda said. She showed me one of the kids' cards. On it was a picture of a scantily clad woman with fairy wings, with tresses of flames. "Like I've told you, Tinsley, this game has played out many times. There is only one way it can end, with me on the pyre or at my rest in the underworld."

I stared at the card. "So we can't just run?"

"No," Leda said. "That's why tomorrow is so important."

"What's going to happen tomorrow at the parade?"

Leda walked out of the rickety house. Once we were out on the street, she turned to me.

"I wouldn't have recovered if we hadn't come upon those children," she said. "They made me a part of their little cult, and it gave me strength. Tomorrow, I will make a new cult, something temporary to help me reclaim the beast and cross over into the underworld."

A car cruised onto the street. When its headlights hit us, the driver honked the horn. Leda took my hand and led me forward urgently.

"We must go quickly."

Once we were settled in the car, I found I couldn't let go of her hand. My thoughts were of life without the beast and the curse of its presence every seven years. The prospect seemed empty. There would be no Leda, or Sandra, or even my postcards.

"Alexandrine's cult knows about the fucking party house," Leda said to Claudio. "Make sure it's cleared out."

He grunted, his eyes watching me through the rearview mirror.

"Tinsley saved my ass today," Leda told him. "She's the beast."

❖

We drove to a motel, a tiny seedy-looking place a bit out of town. Dos Palmas. When we stepped out of the car, I could hear Tejano music blaring from one of the rooms. Leda skipped the check-in desk and led me to a room on the second landing. She opened the door and stepped into the darkened room. When she shut the door, I could only see the silhouettes of the furniture. I sat on the edge of the bed and watched her as she moved around in the dark, shedding her clothes.

I could still hear the music in the distance. After a while, she came to me and straddled my lap. She leaned forward and bit my lip before kissing me there in the dark. Her body felt lithe and feverish under my hands. She broke away from me to turn so that my hands could better reach her more erogenous areas.

I wanted light. I wanted to see her under my hands. My protest came out as a groan. Leda laughed. Her body arched into my touch as I tested the firmness of her belly, the softness of her small breasts cupped in my hands, and the wetness at her center. She locked her legs around my waist and rocked her hips. Each time her ass lifted off my lap and returned, quick pangs of pleasure pulsed from my center.

She moved away from me and stretched out on the bed. I crawled after her and covered her body with mine. She relieved me of my borrowed shirt and played her hands up and down my sore ribs and along my tortured spine. The sighs that escaped her fueled my passion. I pinned her shoulders to the bed and felt her hand slide beneath the waistband of my pants. I parted my legs to give her better access to what she was after.

Her touch was electric. I felt myself slipping away, as if the beast was taking over, except instead of pain, I felt intense pleasure that weakened my limbs, and I could hardly keep myself from falling on top of her.

When I was close to my climax, she began to slide away. I grabbed at her and she laughed at me once again. She climbed off the bed, and for a few agonizing seconds, I lost her to the darkness of the room. My eyes caught a movement near the window where light from the outside bled in through the sides of the curtains.

"Come back," I whispered.

"And what will you do with me?" she asked. I turned around, not able to pinpoint the direction of her voice.

I laughed this time. "You'll have to come back and find out."

"Finish undressing."

I stepped off the bed and did what she asked. Once I was completely naked, I felt Leda slip behind me, her hands on my waist, my belly. She walked in front of me and kneeled. I finally got my wish for light when her eyes began to glow like molten gold, illuminating a circle around us a few feet wide.

She drank deep and the cries that came from my throat startled me.

I sank to the floor with her and kissed a trail from the base of her throat to her abdomen. I sampled the strip of stiff, dark curls, moist from her encounter. She tasted of earth and the air that flowed over the sea, like falling rain, green, and at the same time of the perfumed smoke from a censer.

She cried out, and spoke in that same language from the vision. I felt her reach her climax and took my time releasing her. Her glow faded. She climbed on top of me and kissed my cheek tenderly. Her eyes shimmered in the darkness like faraway stars beneath her closed lids. Even though in so many ways she was like a human woman, from her vices down to the way she snoozed in my arms, she did not belong in this world.

CHAPTER TWELVE

I woke to the sound of female voices chattering over my head. I opened my eyes to see Pearl and Rose standing over me in the dim room. I stirred under the covers, conscious that I wore nothing beneath the sheets. I snaked my arm around the other side of the bed searching for Leda. I turned my neck to find the space empty.

"Whoa," Pearl said. "Someone got it on last night."

"Leave her alone." Rose smiled. "Leda says to feed her and get her ready."

Pearl surreptitiously tossed me the Sun Monster shirt, which I slipped on. Rose brought me a delicious smelling bag of little tacos full of bits of meat, onions, and cilantro. I wolfed down nearly a dozen of them, washed down with a tall bottle of Coke.

"Where is Leda?"

"She's doing a bunch of press for Bacchanista," Pearl said as she unpacked a paper shopping bag from a trendy store.

"Shouldn't I be with her?" I asked.

"We shook the Sisterhood last night," Rose said, sitting on the edge of the bed. "They tried to draw us out of hiding by burning down the party house and Little Foxes."

Pearl shook her head and made an apathetic sound as she

fussed with the clothes from the bag. "There's like an army of them. Throwing Molotov cocktails. All these chicks in black, their faces covered with ninja masks of all things."

I tried to imagine Sandra dressed in such garb tossing a flaming bottle at a smoking house. What Pearl described didn't sound like the Sisterhood I had known, but then again, Juliette was in charge now. Without the beast in their possession, they would have trained to be more proactive.

"They're desperate now," Rose said. "They know it's over for them, after tonight."

"What will you all do when Leda is gone?" I asked.

Rose shrugged. "Maybe go to Hollywood. She's taught us some things."

"How to conquer the cult of fame," Pearl added.

My mind wandered to the Sun Monster kids the night before, how easily she had slipped into their little game, how their admiration had given her strength.

"She said she's making a cult tonight," I mused aloud.

"We better get going," Rose said. "The parade will start in a few hours."

I frowned. "A few hours? Have I been sleeping all day?" They laughed.

"You should feel refreshed," Pearl said. "Now hit the showers."

I put the tee on and slunk to the tiny restroom. Once I was cleaned up, Leda's young witches once again dressed me. This time, they gave me white twill skinny pants embroidered with anchors and a tank top.

As we stepped out into the fading day, I found myself anxious to see Leda, and anxious about the beast who would take over my body in just hours.

We drove to the Montrose district, just minutes away from my home. A resurgence of young professionals had transformed the once exclusively bohemian neighborhood. Restaurants replaced the independent bookstores, and several of the older gay and lesbian bars closed down.

Still, once a year, several blocks were closed down for the Pride festival and parade. Hundreds of revelers usually turned out, and this year was no different. Even on the outskirts of the route, there were throngs of people.

I spotted Claudio standing guard in front of a white tent. A sign at the entrance read *Bacchanist V.I.P. Bash*. Inside the tent, among a small crowd, Leda sat in a director's chair. Her small, shapely body was covered in a silky robe. Despite the humid, sticky air, she waited cool and collected, her eyes covered with dark shades.

She stood to greet me and slowly kissed my cheeks. Her fingers clutched my hand. For a split second, I thought I felt her tremble when we touched.

"Are you ready?" she asked.

I leaned in close to her. "For what exactly?"

She removed her shades. "Just follow my lead. The Sisterhood will try to interfere."

I frowned. "The police are out in full force."

"They'll try," Leda said. She let go of me and moved to walk away. I placed my hand on her arm just above the elbow and held on.

"I'll never see you again."

She smiled. "You haven't become attached, have you?"

Leda came close and kissed me. I clung to her arm, not wanting to let go. Afraid.

"Come on, Tinsley," Pearl said, drawing me away. "Leda's chariot awaits."

I followed them away from the tent and into the bustling gathering. Parade goers set their camps up on small plots along the curb sitting on everything from patio chairs to milk crates. A few of them sat right on the grass drinking, smoking, and snacking.

They were young and old, gay and straight. Most of them were dressed in typical summer wear, but there were a few in proper Pride attire, bikinis and lingerie. I thought of Sandra, the two of us in shorts and tanks in camp chairs. Soon, I would be free of the beast. I could have a life with or without Sandra. The thought didn't bring me much comfort, as I pictured myself just as solitary.

I walked with Leda's witches to the midway point of the route. A row of camp chairs sat in front of a trendy set of resale shops. Several young women welcomed us, and once we were settled, they passed around plastic cups and a thermos of vodka cherry limeade. I sipped my drink quietly and people-watched. The parade started with various council members and the parade marshals in cars that were thumping out the latest pop hits. Houston's lesbian mayor rode past on the back of a convertible and everyone cheered.

The floats started their procession, representing their organizations and businesses with raucous pop music. There were floats for churches, and there were ones for bars and social clubs. Pearl, Rose, and their friends were on their feet, laughing, waving at people they knew on the floats, and snatching at the various trinkets they threw. The witches seemed determined not to let the gravity of whatever was going to happen ruin their mirth. I began to wonder if perhaps, like the party at the old bank, the revelry was part of the rite.

What remained of the day quickly faded to night, leaving only the humidity. Two police officers on motorcycles cruised by and cleared the way for a particularly loud, large float that cruised toward us flashing beams of multicolored light.

It was a bus with the top and seats removed, with a glossy black paint job and the word Bacchanista in a flourished silver, glittery script that matched the website. Men in black cowboy boots and shiny skintight bikini underwear marched in single file on either side with shiny wooden rifles that they tossed and twirled.

A familiar voiced boomed over the music. "Are you ready for the revolution?"

Leda prowled at the top of the bus, a slight, pale figure in the flash of strobe lights. Bandolier belts crisscrossed her bare breasts. She wore rhinestone-covered panties over fishnet stockings and impossibly high-heeled boots. She carried a pink glittering rifle that she lifted into the air and fired. People ducked and cried out in surprise, startled, their faces distorted in a mirthful, giddy, mock fear.

"I said," Leda yelled into a headset mic, "are you motherfuckers ready? Are you ready for *revolución*?"

The crowd cheered.

It was Leda in all her tattooed glory. She grinned triumphantly as she marched around the bus and posed with her rifle for camera phone pics.

I felt a tug on the back of my shirt and turned to see Sandra amongst the crowd of people who had gathered behind us. Her eyes gleamed with determination, and I looked to her hands, sure she would have some kind of weapon, the awful crop and flail perhaps.

Her hands were empty.

"Tinsley," she said. "You've got to get out of here."

By then, the witches had noticed her appearance. They stepped close to me.

"Back off, bitch," Pearl growled.

"You're all in danger," Sandra said, gazing pointedly at me. "Just forget about the Sisterhood, forget that I helped them deceive you, and just walk away from here with me."

"What do you know?" Rose asked.

Sandra spoke again, never looking away from me. "I came here for Tinsley. Not the beast."

Pearl planted a palm on Sandra's shoulder and shoved it. "Get lost, babe. We got things taken care of here."

I moved between them, furious at the young witch. "Don't you touch her."

Sandra ignored the slight. She reached out and snatched one of my hands. "I know you hate me, Tinsley. You let me in and you feel like it was all a lie, but it wasn't."

I looked into her eyes and felt that tug at my heart I felt the day she saw me as the beast in the office restroom, the tenderness she showed, how she slept so peacefully in my arms, the way she looked at me so lovingly when she woke.

"Tinsley."

The black bus had stopped right behind us, and Leda was climbing off a ladder on the back with the aid of a burly man in a full leather mask. He handed her a large black bag, and she reached in and removed a handful of objects. People cheered and reached out their hands over the metal barricades.

"In the old days," Leda said, "people used to drink to relieve themselves of their inhibitions. There was a cult in Rome where people drank themselves mad and fucked whoever they wanted."

Leda handed out a few of the objects in her hands. "Have a drink on me. I am the Bacchanista, and I hope this helps get you guys laid."

Everyone cheered again. She made her way closer, and I saw that her eyes glowed like molten gold. Around us, parade goers were taking the tops off the little clear containers Leda had passed out. The clear plastic gave the appearance of frosted glass etched with the Bacchanista logo. A colorless liquid sloshed around inside. They tossed back the contents of the flasks, and their faces changed. One of the women closest to me let out a whoop and then snarled maniacally, her eyes glazed over. For a brief second, I wondered what was inside the flasks.

Sandra hadn't let go of me. I felt her tug at me, and I turned to look at her. There was an expression of complete sadness on her face.

Leda stopped a few yards away to pose for a picture with the crowd. In the glare of the camera flash, I saw that she wore garish red lipstick, slightly smeared at the corner of her mouth, I suppose, for effect. She was harsh, brash, beautiful, and dangerously waifish. She frightened and aroused me.

Our gazes met and locked. A slight grin tugged at her lips, then vanished. Leda began to march toward me. Her voice boomed over the roar of the crowd and the growl of the bus.

"Tinsley Swan."

Sandra grabbed my arm and gasped. "Tinsley. Let's go."

I shook her off.

"If anyone needs a drink, it's Tinsley," Leda said. "You see, we fucked last night and now her girlfriend is giving her the blues about it."

The crowd booed.

"Poor Tinsley," Leda said and let out an exaggerated sigh. "Even now, she can't decide."

She reached for me, and when I stepped close, she turned to the crowd that had gathered around. She handed out more flasks. She was wrong. I had decided. I would follow her to the underworld if I had to prove it.

Before I could think about this new revelation that had popped into my head, Leda tossed one of the containers at me. I caught it and looked down at the object in my hand. The seven-sided star was embossed onto the plastic.

"Don't drink that shit," Sandra shouted. "Tinsley. Look at everyone around you. This is not going to end well."

"You're no fun." Leda pouted at Sandra. "We'll just have to persuade you differently."

Several people from the crowd surged forward, jostling past me, their eyes empty, though they shouted out lurid things. They caught hold of Sandra, grabbing at her clothes, her arms, and dragging her away. She shouted and fought at them, but there were too many. I stood there. Numb. Watching. I knew it was wrong for those people to have their hands on Sandra. A very small part of me felt her outrage. I turned to Leda. She moved close and reached beneath the wide strap of my tank top. She touched the star above my breast.

"Drink," she demanded.

I only stared at her. The rest of the crowd moved in on a collective breath of anticipation. Music thumped loudly out of the bus. The night around the parade suddenly seemed darker. Somewhere behind me, Sandra screamed.

"Drink," Leda began to chant slowly. "Drink. Drink. Drink."

"Drink. Drink. Drink." People on the sidewalk around us added to the din, and soon so did the people across the street. They climbed over the barricade, startling the horse of a mounted patrol officer. For a split second, something inside me wanted to implore the woman in the blue uniform for help. Of course, there was nothing the cop could do to help. Leda came from a place far beyond her jurisdiction.

I looked back up at Leda. She had stopped chanting and simply watched me. Her gaze burned deep into mine. The noise of the crowd died, replaced by the crackle of fire consuming its fuel. I heard Leda's voice, not in my ear, but in my head, speaking slowly in a language I somehow knew to be long dead. I blinked and saw her face made of fire. She was speaking to me in a guttural voice from the pyre that first night the beast had come upon me.

The roar of the crowd returned. My fingers trembled as I unscrewed the cap. I tossed back my head to dump the drink down my throat. Tequila. A trickle slipped down my windpipe, and I coughed tequila fumes into my lungs. A pain hit me in the gut like a rock-hard fist. I doubled over and felt the muscles in my thighs cramp.

The beast was near.

I stayed down. Leda's impossibly high-heeled dominatrix boots stayed rooted expectantly. I rolled over on my side and saw her smiling down at me. I squirmed to move away. My rib cage rippled beneath my skin, then issued a sickening crunch. Leda planted one of her feet on my stomach and pressed.

"It's time," she said. "Don't fight it, honey."

This was wrong. Leda's parade cult of people who forgot themselves and mobbed one woman. It was all wrong. The change racked my body, and Leda lost her footing. I crawled a few inches and forced myself to stand.

The people around me didn't seem to care that I was changing into a monster. They stood there swaying with the music that emanated from the bus.

"Now don't be like that," Leda said and reached out her hand. "Once I have what is mine, these people will return to normal." When I didn't move, she frowned. "It doesn't matter now. It's all done."

The crowd behind me erupted as Sandra burst through their ranks. "Run, Tinsley," she shouted. "Get out of here."

I bolted, fighting with the transformation as I ran, pressed by the fear of being caught, arrested, or just shot dead in the street by police. As I moved farther away from Leda's bus, I noticed that people were not as zombie-fied as the crowd that dragged Sandra away. Screams punctuated the pulse of music. People, not sure if I was in costume or real, hurried out of my way as I ran down the sidewalk on black-clawed hands and feet. A thunderous groan drowned out the entire melee. The concrete in front of me cracked and bent. I stopped and watched the ground tent in an explosion of broken concrete, dirt, and dust. The fault spread to the street, leveling a float on a trailer being pulled by a pickup. The riders spilled to the ground as the hitch popped loose. The driver of the truck gunned the engine and plowed into another float.

As the riders of the first float recovered and pulled themselves and one another to safety, a manhole cover just a feet away from the overturned trailer shot into the air followed by a column of fire. There were more screams as parade goers ran from the blaze and from me. The manhole cover crashed onto the hood of a parked HPD patrol car, shattering the front windshield.

The fire raged skyward and blazed bright orange on the edges, black at the center, a hazy blue film in the middle. It was no ordinary blaze; neither was it the Sacred Fire.

I backed away from the scene and down a narrow alleyway between a thrift store and a bar. It was about as wide as my shoulders; the brick walls were slick with slime in places where the building's AC dripped, and tufts of grass grew between cracks in the concrete. I disturbed a stray cat that hissed and scampered away.

In the darkness, I hunkered down, exhausted and confused. It was too late to get back home to lock myself away. The cycle of my curse had come to its end, and I was beginning to slip away, my body giving way to the beast's.

Screaming, shouts, and sirens carried into the alley as the darkness in my mind became one with the darkness around me. A wind gathered in the small space of the alleyway. The smell of scorched earth and sulfur carried to my nostrils. The wind strengthened to gale that shook the brick walls of the buildings on either side of me. I stayed close to the ground battered by the foul, dry air. The wind pressed against me like probing hands, rolling over my torso and neck. Those unseen hands pried past my lips and inflated my lungs to over capacity.

My body rose several inches. I gripped at the concrete with now-clawless hands. The air rushed from my lungs and swirled before me in the form of a black cloud. I blinked my watering eyes as the cloud took on a familiar shape.

There, standing nose-to-nose with me, was the beast. Flame-colored eyes stared at me beneath red fur, illuminating the face.

Seven horns crowned the head and studded gray scaly patches of skin were between the eyes and on the muzzle. The coal-black nose snorted out a stream of hot breath.

Without my body to hinder it, the beast stood taller and wider. It could barely negotiate its way out of the alley toward the chaos beyond, a reptilian tail trailing behind. Once free of the confines of the two buildings, the beast shook itself and disappeared into the fiery doom beyond.

I watched it go and for a moment a mix of elation and relief passed through me. Leda had freed me of the beast. It was gone. I stood there in the darkness, listening to the sound of my own breathing. I had not expected such carnage and destruction. I certainly didn't expect innocent people to be drawn into Leda's plans or an explosion in the middle of the Pride parade. Then there was the matter of Sandra being dragged away by a mob. Now the beast was loose on its own.

Something was terribly wrong.

"Tinsley!"

I straightened and sudden tears stung my eyes. Sandra was close by. I limped toward the mouth of the alley and realized that the transformation had shredded my clothes.

In the time since I had left the scene, things had deteriorated greatly. The great fire still roared from the manhole, the black center dilating like the pupil of some massive eye. A few cops ran among the chaos, determined to get people to safety, but the former parade goers had dissolved into something else. A group of men and women gathered beneath a streetlight sang a ribald pop song as they swigged from bottles of wine with various labels. Other revelers had paired off and were making love in the street and on the sidewalks.

Among them walked Sandra. I waved to her weakly, and she ran toward me, a look of relief on her face. As she neared, she saw the tears on my face and opened her arms.

I backed away, into the darkness of the alley.

"What have I done?" I asked.

"It's not over yet," Sandra said, taking my hand. "We have to get to Salacia."

When she tugged my hand, I didn't budge.

"Come on, Tinsley," she said. "It's a matter of life or apocalypse here."

She noticed my near nakedness and darted out of the alley. I watched her gather several articles of clothing from the more amorous of what remained of the parade goers. She returned and pressed them on me.

"Get dressed," she said and reached out to touch my face.

I shook my head.

"What are you going to do?" she asked. "Stay here and watch it all burn?"

I didn't say a word, let the borrowed clothes fall at my feet.

"Oh, hell no," Sandra said. "You put those fucking clothes on, Tinsley Swan. Then you can go back to your work and your sad, lonely life. I promise."

Her words shocked me. "It was fine before you came and tampered with it."

Sandra narrowed her eyes. "You don't get it, do you? Your life was what your precious goddess wanted it to be. Hopefully, when that bitch is burned at the stake, you'll see that."

She reached into the pocket of the black cargo pants she wore and removed her phone.

"I've got her," Sandra said in greeting. "We're right at the fire."

In the glow of the phone, I saw her eyes widen. "Oh. Shit."

She turned to me, the cell to her ear. "Yeah. No. We're going to hang out here for a second."

Sandra placed the phone back in her pocket and grabbed my hand again. She dragged me to the edge of the alley and pointed at the column of fire. After a few seconds, the beast appeared galloping on all fours, with Leda on its back. The Lost Goddess sat as poised as a dressage rider, her lipstick still artfully smeared, her hair a fearsome halo.

The beast ran toward the blazing column of fire and did not slow as it approached the burning obstacle. The beast bowled over a police officer attempting to rope off the scene with tape, knocking her to the street. The beast lowered its head, leapt over a mating couple, and soared into the black center.

The fiery eye wavered a bit like a candle flame stirred by breath, but otherwise remained unmoved. Leda and the beast did not reappear on the other side.

Sandra turned to me. "See? She's gone, Tinsley, and things are still shitty, and it's going to get worse unless we haul ass to Salacia."

As she spoke, the giant flame wavered again. A dark shape lumbered forth. At first, its form seemed simian, but the jutting lower jaw and fangs told of something far more sinister. It tripped forward cautiously, unsure of its new surroundings.

"Fuck." Sandra shoved me back into the alley. I scrambled in the dark for the clothing she had given me earlier.

"What is that thing?" I asked as I shed the torn garments given to me by Leda's witches earlier. It seemed ages ago.

"It's a gallu," she said, "Demons that roam the outer ring of the underworld. They'll be the first to know of the breach. According to the wisdom, they are easier to kill."

Dressed, I straightened. "No one told me anything about demons." As we stepped out of the alley, I saw that the thing Sandra had called a gallu was sniffing at a stupefied reveler who stumbled up the street unaware of what exactly stalked her. A car horn honked and a black sedan careened forward, dodging the parade debris of overturned trailers and prone bodies.

The reveler had enough sense to stumble out of the way as she made some obscene gesture. The gallu only turned and sniffed at the headlights. The car struck the creature head-on. The thing disintegrated into a cloud of ash and burning embers.

Juliette, along with four other women in black, exited the car. Sandra dragged me to them.

"We've got our work cut out for us tonight," Juliette said, eyeing me shrewdly. She looked to the others and began to give instructions.

"Rally everyone at this point," she said. "Kill anything that comes out of there. When the cops show up, I want you to fall back, but keep an eye on things."

To my surprise, their faces were young, their eyes glued to their leader. This was a far cry from Aunt Quinn and those spoiled, squabbling old biddies I remembered from the summer of '83. Juliette instructed them with brisk care. She then turned to us and touched Sandra's shoulder.

"Are we ready?"

"Yeah," Sandra said. She guided me to the car. As we climbed in, several excited shouts rang out as another gallu exited the fire. Before any of the others could react, Juliette pulled out a cannon of a gun with a silencer on the end. She fired on the thing, and just like the other, it broke into smoldering pieces.

Sandra slid on her seat belt. "We've got to go."

Juliette plunked herself behind the wheel. "I had always hoped it would never come to this. All the training in the world couldn't prepare them for this." She looked in the rearview mirror at me. "This is what you wanted, Tinsley."

"Stop it," Sandra told her. "It's not all her fault."

Juliette began to back the car away from the fiery eye. "It is my fault," I said in a voice so small, I didn't recognize it as my own.

Sandra turned to look at me. "Let's just all cut out the whining for now." As we made our way off the parade route, two completely naked woman frolicked past the headlights and into the darkness.

"Damn," Sandra said. "They're having a time."

CHAPTER THIRTEEN

We drove at a breakneck speed down I-45 to Galveston. Juliette and Sandra explained to me that they were going to get the beast back in our custody.

"You mean back in me," I said.

"It has to be you," Juliette said. "We can't risk channeling the beast into anyone else."

"What if this is it?" I asked Juliette. "Leda gets to go back to the underworld, and a few demons get loose."

"Not according to Alexandrine," Sandra said. "It seems Leda was the only thing trying to get into the underworld. Everything else apparently wants out."

I felt my hands ball into fists. "Leda promised to free me of the beast, a chance at a normal life. It was more hope than I had in a long time."

I glanced at Sandra. That last bit had been a lie. That afternoon she walked into the ladies' room and saw the beast and did not turn away had given me more hope than Leda's promises.

"Of course it never occurred to you that she might be lying," Juliette snarled. "You only think of yourself, Tinsley."

"Myself is all I've had," I countered.

"You made that choice."

"I never would have agreed to anything if I had known people would be hurt and there would be so much property damage."

"Maybe you should have fucking listened."

"Girls," Sandra interjected.

"You're in love with her," Juliette scoffed at her. "It's obvious that she's not into the Sisterhood, and you're still in love with her."

"Just shut up, Juliette," Sandra growled as she dug around in the glove compartment. She turned and kneeled in the seat to present me with a gun as big as Juliette's.

I shrank away.

"Just point and shoot," she said, balancing it on my leg.

"You don't expect me to know how to use this after a four-word instructional course?"

Sandra reclaimed the gun and flicked a little switch near the top of the handle two times. She once again proffered the cannon in her open hand.

"Safety. That's five words."

I took the gun and she patted my leg reassuringly.

Our first stop was the Palm and Oak Cemetery, the oldest one in Galveston. A long gravel drive lined with towering pines led up to the wrought iron black gates. Juliette cut the chains with something shiny and furtive. She led us through the cemetery just as Quinn had led the procession of the Sisterhood back in '83. Juliette, all business, carried a flat piece of metal under her arm. We crossed through rows of tops of mausoleums lost when the city was leveled after the hurricane of 1900. We stopped in front of the winged woman who guarded the door to the stone building with the placard that read Tinsley.

Sandra shined the flashlight on her phone, and the stone angel's roman features angled in the brightness.

"Fire," I said. "This statue is not of a winged woman. She is wreathed in flame." I touched Juliette's shoulder. "Why have we come to Alexandrine's tomb?"

"Actually," Juliette said. "No one is buried here."

Sandra and I glanced at each other as she slid the bar alongside the door until something on the other side clicked audibly. She pushed the door and it glided away as if on casters. She stepped aside.

"You should go first, Tinsley," Juliette said. "This is your birthright."

Her words made me pause. Sandra took my hand and gave me a smile of reassurance. I led the way down a low, narrow passageway. After a few steps, I noticed a dancing glow and moving shadows up ahead. I heard voices. My foot caught on a deep crack in the floor, and I reached for the wall to steady myself. The walls had changed from smooth stone to rough and damp. Sandra's hand covered mine.

"Texas limestone," she commented.

She tilted her head up. I did so as well and saw that the ceiling was made of roughly hewn branches and palm fronds in a thatched fashion. We made our way to the end of the short corridor and into an airy room.

Seven women waited inside the mausoleum. They wore dark full skirts that swept the floor and white aprons, most of which were torn and stained. One woman languished on the floor. She lay on her stomach. Her dress had been burned away at her back, revealing heavily blistered skin. Three women attended her, held on to her as if they held her very soul in her body.

They all looked at me as one, then at each other.

One of them stood and crossed the small space. She stood tall in a black dress. The apron was made out of a tight metal mesh. Chain mail. Her hair fell in curls as dark as her dress. She took my hand and spoke to me in French. I could only pick out one word: *Fille*. The woman, who looked only to be a few years older than I was, called me daughter.

"She knows who you are," Juliette said.

"What is this place?" I asked.

"English," the woman said. "Yes, of course. What is your name?"

"Tinsley Swan," I said. "Do you live in here?"

"It is a spell," she said. "Time is frozen here in this crypt so that my daughters may always seek my counsel."

Sandra touched my shoulder. "Oh my God, we've gone back in time."

I looked to Juliette. She gave me a wry smile. She stepped past me and reached for the tall woman's hand.

"Tinsley, this is Alexandrine D'Orleans," she said. "Quinn told me exactly what was in here before she died."

"What year is this?" I asked the tall woman, my ancestor.

"Seventeen ninety-two," Alexandrine said. "We brought the incarnation of the goddess across the ocean, to the land beyond the Indies, to destroy her once and for all." She motioned to her fallen sister. "We have nearly failed, and the gallu were almost too much for us. We made the decision to sacrifice ourselves here, to remain in this time and place."

"The barrier to the underworld has been broken before?" I asked.

"Yes," Alexandrine said. "And it will be opened again. It is up to the Sisterhood to close it each time."

"We have lost possession of the beast," Juliette said. "The generation before us was careless and extravagant. At the first sight of trouble, they scattered to the wind."

Alexandrine looked alarmed for a few seconds, then her serene smile returned. "As long as one of the Sisterhood breathes a loyal breath then the wisdom lives. The goddess must never be allowed to stay in the underworld long enough to pass through the seventh gate."

"What do we have to do?" I asked.

She smiled again and motioned for the rest of the Sisters to stand. They did, two of them helping the wounded one, groaning, to her feet. Alexandrine walked a circle around me, her eyes gleaming.

She stopped and removed her chain mail apron and her dress. One of the Sisters assisted her with removing her stays. Suddenly, she gasped and doubled over. She slipped off her shift and fell to the muddy floor on her knees.

She was changing. It was strange to see it happen to someone else, but no less gruesome. Seven short, crooked horns sprouted from her head. She moaned as her rib cage rippled and expanded. She reached for me, and I took her clawed hand.

Blackness claimed my vision. I saw the beast galloping through a strange landscape of skeletal trees barren of leaves beneath a blood-red sky randomly blackened by fast-moving clouds. Leda clung to the beast's back. She leaned forward, her eyes narrowed, her brow furrowed with the intensity of a jockey. They approached a ring of stones. Leda fell hard to the dusty ground. The beast had vanished beneath her. Leda roared, her glowing skin brightening until flames sprang forward.

The light returned, and there stood Alexandrine, her dress torn from the change. The six other sisters helped her to her feet.

"Won't this change anything?" I asked.

"No," Alexandrine said, out of breath. "Time is a trifle to the old ones, Tinsley."

"How do you know this?"

"Because my blood is pure," she said, "The fire there is only a spark, yet the wisdom will never die. Carry it with you until the end."

I stooped and helped her to her stand. The Sisters came and clothed her again. Their attentions seemed to give her strength.

"Go," she said. "Put things right."

Sandra was in a deep conversation with a red-haired woman. They spoke slowly in Spanish, as their dialects were an ocean and several centuries apart. The woman handed Sandra a blue velvet pouch with a black braided drawstring. Sandra opened the bag and reached her hand in. She gasped and pulled out a large deck of cards. She fanned them out expertly as she searched the faces around her.

"Tinsley, these look just like my cards."

I looked to the red-haired woman who reached out and touched the ends of Sandra's hair. She seemed to marvel at its coloring. When Sandra tried to give the cards back, she refused them.

After a round of embraces, Juliette led us back out into the night. I glanced at my watch. I had checked it just as we entered. We had only spent about two minutes inside the mausoleum, yet it felt as if at least twenty minutes had elapsed. There was still time.

I reached out in the darkness and caught hold of Sandra's hand. If there was ever a question in my mind of whether I could love her, it was gone way before I discovered she was one of the Sisterhood. I wanted to tell her.

"I slept with Leda," I blurted.

"Tinsley," Sandra said, peering at me through the night. "I figured you would."

"I'm sorry," I said.

"You're an idiot," she said simply.

In front of us, Juliette slowed her walk to a stop and motioned for us to do the same.

"What is it?" I asked.

"Quiet," Juliette hissed out a whisper.

She removed her gun from the holster strapped to her thigh.

I held on tight to Sandra's hand as I followed the direction of Juliette's gaze to the shadows of a sprawling oak that melded with the shadows of several monuments. After a few seconds, my eyes picked out what looked to be twin red-hot embers floating in the darkness. The embers moved, and I saw the outline of a body, back hunched, low to the ground, the protruding jaw that yawned low as the creature opened its mouth.

"We must have done something right," Sandra whispered.

"Let's walk," Juliette growled. "When I tell you to get down, I need you two to hit the dirt."

She moved quickly up the path, Sandra and I close behind.

We continued to move toward the gates we had slipped through earlier. I tried to call upon the beast, but the pains of transformation would not come. I wondered if Alexandrine's transference had worked. Sandra's hand tightened around my fingers in a death grip.

The creature began to rock on its stout back legs. It lunged, launching itself several feet into the air in a noiseless leap. Juliette shouted for us to get down.

Sandra dragged me to the ground as gunshots thundered. The creature's head exploded into glowing ash and hellish debris that rained all over us. Juliette urged us on, coughing as we went.

We slipped through the gate and climbed into the car, Sandra and I in the backseat, Juliette in the driver's seat. I retrieved the gun I had left behind, my hands shaking. I looked around at the faces of my companions in the interior light of the car. The fear and strain showed in their darting eyes, the tightness of their lips.

Juliette spoke. "Let's get the hell out of here."

She turned on the engine and flicked on the headlights. The night before us lit up, revealing a beast about the size of a rhino, but hyena-like in its look and movements. Like the other gallu, it had large eyes like burning coals.

Sandra cried out, her alarm cut short by the shriek of tires. We were thrown forward into the backs of the front seats as the car began to speed away in reverse. The creature let out a raspy bellow and galloped forward on its stout legs, quickly gaining speed with each step.

The car hurtled backward down the long gravel drive toward the main road. Juliette wrapped her arm around the back of the headrest on the passenger side, then looked over her shoulder and past us to the night beyond the back windshield. The monster thundered closer, and in the glare of the headlights, I could make out every detail of its visage from the freakishly long snout, to the long ivory fangs curled up on either side in a snarl. The bottom half of the muzzle fell open, revealing double rows of jagged teeth.

"When we get to the road, shoot it," Juliette said. "Sandra, you first. If you can't take it out, Tinsley will join in."

I nodded dumbly, sure that it was pointless to remind her I had never fired a gun in my life and of all the things that could possibly go wrong.

She seemed to sense my doubt, and for a second, rolled her eyes from the back windshield to stare directly at me.

"That thing could topple the car if it hits us."

Sandra rolled down the passenger window and took hold of the gun she carried. The moist air of the humid July night brought the scent of burning coal and sulfur. The fabled smell of brimstone. I removed the safety of my own gun, as Sandra had instructed during her very short training session earlier.

Sandra reached over and touched my face and moved away as if to give me space. That brief gesture assured me more than any words she could have spoken.

The car tilted backward, and we were jostled as the drive ended in a steep slope and gravel transitioned to pavement. Sandra leaned out the window and fired on the thing, once, twice, three times before we turned onto the street. As we drove away, I could see it stamping and shaking off the bullets as if they were ants.

"I think it's off our tail," I said.

In the rearview mirror, Juliette smirked, pleased with Sandra's shooting. I wondered what other camaraderie they shared.

The car lurched forward, the tires squealing as we were struck from behind. I turned to see the demon that had chased us out of the cemetery galloping close enough to ram us once more with its massive head.

"Shit," Sandra shrieked. "We're going to need your help, Tinsley."

"Empty your clips," Juliette barked. "Make every shot count."

I leaned out the window and fired at the gallu that pursued us. The interior of the car thundered with each pull of the trigger. I gritted my teeth and continued to fire at the thing's face. The bullets pierced the demon's hide, leaving burning holes. The wounds hardly fazed the demon at first, but my aim got better with each shot, and a chunk of its muzzle fell to the ground and was trampled under black claws.

The town unfolded around us in silhouette backlit by orange streetlights. The sound of gunshots would bring attention. The thought alarmed me, but perhaps if a police officer saw a two-ton demon chasing after us, they would join in.

My arms trembled from the recoil. My hands were sweaty and the gun felt like a slippery fish. It took all my will to continue holding it and firing. The creature kept pace with the car, a black liquid trailing from its damaged mouth. It exhaled a cloud of sparks that showered the dark street.

I stopped squeezing the trigger and watched as the demon's head began to dissolve in clumps of burning debris. There were more sparks, and a mist of ash floated in through the broken back window.

The creature fell and crackled like the remains of a burned-out log reduced to glowing cinders. Sandra turned to lean against the seat in relief. I joined her and we leaned together, shoulder to shoulder. In the rearview mirror, I saw Juliette's eyes. No longer so intent on driving, she dialed someone on her cell and told them we were close. She ended the call and told us that the pyre was ready.

"All we need is the Lost Goddess."

The car slowed as we came to the mouth of the white gravel drive that led to Salacia. Once we passed through the gates, a speeding red form collided with the driver's side of the sedan. Sandra and I were thrown against each other and into the passenger door panel.

The car bounced and slid sideways several feet in a cacophony of shattering glass, tortured fiberglass, and bending metal, then came to a grinding halt. I glanced around and saw Juliette still buckled in. She was slumped over at the waist; her torso was across the center console, and her head was angled toward the passenger seat.

Next to me, Sandra groaned and fumbled around in the dark. She popped open the door and called my name weakly before stumbling onto the street. I followed and stopped to look around to see what hit us. Over the hood of the car, I saw Jimmy's van, the front end wrecked, the engine hissing white smoke. His crooked form sat still behind the driver's seat. The bastard had hit us.

"What are you doing?" I shouted.

He didn't answer.

"You son of a bitch, you could have killed us."

Sandra grabbed the sleeve of my shirt. "Juliette."

I opened the front passenger door, leaned in, and touched Juliette's neck. I felt her pulse still strong and steady. I patted her face gently to wake her. I kneeled on the seat, reached over, and unbuckled her belt. To my relief, she stirred beneath me. I whispered her name.

"We were hit," she said.

"Jimmy, my antique dealer, ex-antique dealer."

She grinned. At least her sense of humor was still intact.

"We have to get out of here. Are you hurt?"

She nodded. "I think so."

Behind us, in the backseat, Sandra gathered the blue bag

from the mausoleum and the gun, which had fallen under the passenger seat in the melee.

"Everything okay?" she asked. In the dying glow of the dashboard, I checked Juliette for injuries. A nasty bruise began to spread at her jaw, across her cheek. I touched her face gently.

"Tinsley?"

"Yeah?"

"I've loved you, all this time."

I glanced over my shoulder at Sandra, who stood outside the car keeping watch. I looked back to Juliette, who smiled wanly and nodded. We had both in different ways given our lives to the Sisterhood. Looking into her eyes, I knew that she had held on to the memories of the summer of '83 as I had.

"Let's get you out of here."

I helped her out of the car and onto the street. She winced and gasped when she tried to stand on her own. Sandra wrapped her arm around Juliette's waist to steady her.

"It's my leg." Juliette touched the side of her left thigh gingerly. "It's broken."

"We need to get to the pyre," she groaned, and lost her footing. Sandra stumbled under the sudden weight. I managed to keep them from falling. We hitched along toward the house. I saw the glow of the Sacred Fire and the silhouette of the house flickering in the light.

Halfway up the white drive, Sandra stopped us. She peered anxiously at the shadows between the oaks on the side. "There's one out there watching us."

I peered into the darkness until I could make out the misshapen form, lurking, prowling, its glowing eyes concentrating on our little huddle.

"Hold on to her," Sandra said, transferring Juliette's weight to me.

She shot at the thing and it darted away only to be replaced by two more. I fired. The light from the discharge of the gun revealed a half dozen of the creatures waiting in the darkness.

"They're everywhere," Sandra gasped.

"Did they follow us from Houston?" I asked.

"Once the Sisterhood started the Sacred Fire, the hell gate should have closed," Juliette wheezed. "These must have slipped through on this side."

"We need the beast," Sandra said urgently. "Tinsley—"

"I know," I shouted. "The mausoleum…it must not have worked."

A warm body bowled into my back. I fell forward on my hands and knees. The gun clattered to the road and skipped a few feet away. Sandra's and Juliette's well-being dominated the jumble of thoughts that burned in my brain as I hit the gravel. I heard their startled screams.

Before I could turn over, a weight settled on my back, pressing me into the rocks. Sharp claws dug into the skin at my ribs. Hot, foul breath assaulted my neck and teeth dug into either side of my left shoulder.

I struggled to get up, but it seemed to set the teeth deeper into my skin, through sinew and cartilage. I screamed, bile rising into the back of my throat. One gun blast rang out into the night, and a second blast sent the gallu on my back flying.

I sat up in a shower of sparks and embers. To my right, Juliette sat on the driveway shooting the demons that slipped out of the shadows beyond the road, their eyes aglow with hellfire. She swung the gun toward me and I turned to my left to see Sandra swatting at one of the demons with her bag of tarot cards. Its teeth snagged on the fabric, tearing a hole in the bag and sending cards flying. There were sparks, and the thing shrieked and backed away. Juliette shot it back into the oblivion it came from.

One of the gallu slowly stalked behind her. She pivoted at the waist and shot the thing. Another leapt out of darkness and snapped onto her injured leg. She screamed and aimed her gun. It didn't fire. She was out of ammo. She flung her gun at the thing. It yelped out a swarm of sparks before bursting into flames. She shielded her face from the flash. She then removed a retractable baton from her boot, ready for the next attack.

I looked back to Sandra and saw that she was making a circle around herself with the cards. I puzzled at her action until I saw one of the gallu leap forward and explode in sparks and ash. Inside the circle, Sandra crossed her arms over her face. She called to me and Juliette to join her.

I stood and went to help Juliette, dodging one of the leaping demons. I kicked at the one that had bitten Juliette's leg. It prowled around her, growling. Another joined it. Beyond the shadows, I happened to see the crooked figure of a man. Jimmy.

"Help us," I shouted at him.

To my relief, Jimmy limped out of the shadows toward us with a tire iron in his hand. I helped Juliette to her feet. Together, we limped toward Sandra's circle. Behind us, Jimmy fended off the gallu.

I delivered Juliette to the circle. I turned to check on Jimmy and saw that he was surrounded. A familiar pain claimed my stomach and back. I rolled over into a ball and felt the beast claim my body. The change doubled me over, but I welcomed it, welcomed that pain. One of the demons leapt at me and I swatted it away with a half-clawed hand. It fell and exploded into a pool of embers.

Jimmy screamed. Two of the things had hold of his arms. They pulled him to the street and savaged him. I charged and tossed the gallu aside like trash. Jimmy looked up at me with a mixture of fear and awe. I howled at the sky in triumph.

A searing wind rolled around me. The night began to lighten as it was suffused with an unknown glow. I looked around for the source of the light. It grew brighter. I saw the outline of a figure in the glow, made completely of fire.

Leda.

She moved fast, a corona of flames around her head and a blazing tail behind her like a comet. She rushed me. The intense heat knocked me to the street, and Leda was on top of me burning as bright as a star. Her face had no features.

"Tinsley, I will take you with me to my slumber. I will return, while you will not see this life or Sandra again."

She burned white hot, bleaching the night, burning my eyes.

Leda was right, but I had not failed, not totally. I had bought the world another seventy years. Juliette and the Sisterhood would continue. The cycle of seven would continue. I closed my eyes and waited for the fire of Leda to consume me.

Instead of darkness, when I closed my eyes, there was a blood-red glow.

I saw a cavern flowing with black rushing water, and beneath were the ethereal blue forms of floating, glowing bodies. There were shadows of expressions on their faces, some completely serene, others in agony. Above the surface, a familiar face appeared. She looked a little older, though I would never tell her. Sandra, searching with a flashlight, the corners of her mouth pulled up in an excited grin. From the water, she pulled a dripping metallic cup engraved with a crop and flail. She turned it around to reveal a seven-sided star.

"Tinsley, I think this is it."

I opened my eyes. Leda's white light faltered, and I knew she too had seen my vision and had some knowledge of its meaning. The shadow of a woman's figure played over us, standing on splayed legs, and one arm was raised over its head, some kind of stick in her hand. I recognized the form as Juliette. She had a crop in one hand, the flail in the other. She stepped fully into the light. I saw perspiration and tears on her cheeks and her brow creased in pain. I tried to warn her away, but only a whimpering bark came out. I doubt she would have listened to me at that point.

She lashed out at the fiery form. One of the gallu appeared out of nowhere and collided with her. She fell from my view.

I summoned my strength and managed to push Leda away, just an inch. She faltered and floated backward, taking the light with her. I tore at her with black claws. What remained of the light burned, but I continued to claw until it cooled.

The white light died, leaving only the night. The gallu were all gone. Jimmy sat in the middle of the street holding his bleeding shoulder, dazed. I stood and saw Juliette lying in the street, her body wreathed in smoke. A few feet away lay Leda, still glowing lightly, but steadily fading.

Six women jogged up the gravel path shining white beams from flashlights. They surveyed the scene and a few of them came to kneel beside Juliette. The rest of them stood over Leda's prone form. I took a tentative step toward the fallen goddess.

Sandra came to me and embraced me. "She wants to talk to you."

Together, we went to Juliette. She lay on her side, barely breathing. She reached up. Sandra kneeled next to her and touched her face.

I loomed in close, my body hulking over the Sisterhood, Sandra, and Juliette.

She smiled when she saw me.

"Tinsley, you and Sandra must lead them now."

I chuffed in affirmative.

"Thank you," she said. "Both of you."

She closed her eyes and breathed her last. I pressed my face against hers, sniffed the last remnants of her life as they gave way to the beginnings of decay. I placed a clawed paw gently on her chest. For years, I had felt guilt for hurting her while in the form of the beast.

"It's time to finish this," Sandra said.

The Sisterhood lifted Leda on their shoulders. They began to march toward the house and the pyre that burned in the distance.

Sandra and I fell behind them, while Jimmy brought up the rear of our grim procession.

We reached the yard where more of the Sisterhood members waited. I wondered how many of them there were, how many would look up to me. I realized then that it must have been past midnight and there I stood before the Sacred Fire as the beast, yet fully conscious of myself and the road before me.

Sandra stopped and held on to me, urging me to stop as well. I did. We watched the Sisterhood approach the burning pyre. Unlike the fire in Houston, it looked like any other bonfire on a humid summer night, except the roar of the flames was like a million voices calling across time.

The din of the Sacred Fire grew louder as the Sisterhood grew near, and two tendrils of flame stretched out like arms for the burden they carried. Leda began to thrash weakly, her glowing body flashing like coals stirred by a wind. She fell to the ground and clawed at the dark grass, screaming. I moved to help her. Sandra tugged at me sternly, her face haunted by the scene.

"Let her go, Tinsley," she said.

The Sisterhood caught hold of Leda's waist, her arms. Brutally, they dragged her toward the pyre. Leda continued to fight with them. She screamed and it sounded like a chorus of women in the throes of agony. Once again, I felt compelled to help her. I moved toward the melee, but Sandra held on to me, her fingers tangled deep in my fur.

Visions like the one from the chiminea seized my brain, and I was assaulted by those old sounds and smells as well as sights. I saw Leda lashed to the mast of a ship, calling out for me, her familiar, in that old language.

The reaching flames coiled around Leda's legs and dragged her across the grass. We watched as the fire pulled her into its depths. A chorus of growls echoed around us. She screamed once again, and I joined her with a sad howl. Sandra let go of the tufts of fur at my shoulders. She studied me in the light of the blaze and then swiftly hugged me around the neck without further hesitation. I knew then that she loved me.

An explosion shattered our short-lived calm.

From the pyre, a ball of flame barreled across the lawn, right past us. I felt the heat of the fire on my face as I urged Sandra away. A thundering crash followed. I looked up to see my family home and the gaping, smoldering hole straight through the west side. Fire roared from the gap, and the comet shot out toward us once again. The Great Pyre roared one last time and died in a hiss of smoke.

One of the Sisterhood members touched my fur-covered shoulder. "We have a car. You two must leave here. We'll take care of everything else."

Another of the young women collected Jimmy and his van. Our eyes met as he passed. I saw regret and sorrow on his face. As far as he knew, Leda was gone, forever.

I knew better.

A black car pulled up, and a member of the Sisterhood climbed out so Sandra could drive me home. I lay down in the backseat. As we sped away from Salacia, Sandra would occasionally reach back between the seats to pet me absentmindedly, running her fingers through the fur on my back.

❖

Once home, I went straight upstairs, nudged the rolltop away, and pushed the seamless door open to the secret room with its padded walls. Sandra came behind me, spied what I had revealed, and shook her head.

"No, Tinsley. You don't have to hide yourself away. You're in control of the beast. You won't hurt me or anyone else."

That said, she left the secret room, the door ajar. I waited. Listened. I heard the shower. When I ventured out, she was wrapped in my robe, her hair damp. She smiled when she saw me and hugged me around the neck. I cradled her close, careful of the horns and the claws. She smelled of good, subtle things like fruit and flowers. Her pulse quickened before steadying again.

She moved away from me and went to the bedroom. I trailed far behind and watched from the doorway as she climbed under the covers. She waved me over and I sat on the floor next to her.

"Rest with me," she said.

I laid my horned head on the mattress but stayed on the floor. I watched her sleep. Time elapsed differently as the beast. The light in the room changed around my vigil, and she opened her eyes. I shadowed her as she dressed in one of my T-shirts and a pair of my yoga pants. She then went downstairs and scrambled an entire carton of eggs and turned on the television. All of the morning shows were all abuzz about the riot at the Houston Pride parade. Footage of the aftermath played on every channel. Luckily, all of the parade goers were too terrified or deep under Leda's spell to take cell phone videos. There was already talk of canceling next year's Pride parade, and a backlash against the rumor.

"They have no idea of the danger we truly faced," Sandra said as she set breakfast on the table. "I'll leave the TV on to keep you company while I'm at work."

The sentiment and the tone of her voice made me feel like a very old dog. I head-butted the television over the back of the stand, killing the insipid daytime show voices that chattered from it.

"The fuck?" Sandra asked. She palmed the side of her face. "You could have humored me, you know. I don't want to leave you either, but the both of us can't be out all week."

I hunched over my mound of eggs and sulked, though it actually felt good to destroy stuff and know I was still in control enough not to hurt Sandra or anyone else.

She came and patted my shoulder before she left.

"I refuse to clean up that mess with the TV."

She left me. I rambled around the house. I peeked out the window and watched Bobby and his friends play in the glaring sunlight. If things had played out differently the night before, those kids could have been killed by gallu. I was relieved to see the world was right again. Like the Sisterhood, their little cult continued. The sun rose high around them.

Before I knew it, the gate opened and Sandra's car pulled into the driveway. I waited by the door until she entered with a bag of food. She wore a short sundress, and sunglasses perched on top of her head.

"I brought steaks and potatoes," she sang.

She placed the containers on the table and opened them before I could attempt to tear through the plastic with my claws.

"Don't worry about work," she said. "We'll get through the week, and this will be behind us for the next seven years."

I snorted.

"Well, you owe me a trip." She grinned as she cut at her steak. "I was thinking we should meet with the Sisterhood. I can finally get the mark."

Another snort from me. Apart from one particular member, the thought of the Sisterhood didn't thrill me. Even after the events that had taken place in the last twenty-four hours.

Sandra sighed. "They're taking Juliette back to France. We'll have to go and visit her grave. I met her shortly after the whole Tinsley Swan debacle. I was in love with her from day one, but of course, she was too involved with the Sisterhood."

As she walked toward the door to leave, I crept behind and carefully nuzzled her back. I wanted to tell her that once I was "normal" we could do and go wherever she wanted, that I was sorry about Juliette's death, that I had forgiven her for her initial deceit, that I would forgive her anything.

She turned to me and smiled. I realized then that I didn't need to be able to speak to tell her of my gratitude, my love. She looked into my eyes, past the beast, and saw.

EPILOGUE: 2081

Bobby took her time negotiating the street. She didn't walk a straight path on the sidewalk but ambled on the curb in between parked cars and along shop windows. The reason for her erratic stroll came rolling down the street on its own track. A domed patrol unit whirred close, its tiny blue and red light flashing around in a circle. It also sported a high-powered floodlight rigged with motion sensors and a camera that recorded all it saw.

The streets of this part of town were much too dangerous for patrol officers after dark. The curfew evened things out. Anyone caught by a unit on the streets after dark was assessed a two-hundred-dollar fine. More than a week's salary for most of the people in this neighborhood.

Bobby imagined she would have grown up in a neighborhood like this if it weren't for the Sisterhood. Her grandfather, whom she was named for, lived in such a place when things were slightly better. If it weren't for Tinsley Swan, Bobby, the child of a convict father and a bitter, alcoholic mother, probably would never have left this neighborhood of dilapidated houses.

She stepped out onto the street once the unit passed. She touched her earpiece.

"All clear. Bring the car around."

She crossed over to a fenced-in lot. A man came out to meet her. He dressed in the way common people imagined the "haves" dressed. He wore a silky top hat and a striped tuxedo jacket over a cheap jersey shirt and sport pants tucked into boots. He didn't say a word as she passed him a wad of bills as big as her fist.

"That covers the backstage visit as well," she told him. "And my employer has brought a gift for the star: a vintage tequila."

The man smacked his lips. "I'll have to have a toast."

"My employer would not be pleased," Bobby told him.

He chuckled. "You not from 'round here, are you?"

The car pulled up then, a sleek four-door sedan. She checked the street and opened the door. Tinsley Swan eased out of the car and straightened. Though she leaned on a cane, she still stood as tall as most men. Her silver-white hair was perfectly coifed. She carried a blue velvet bag.

How thrilled Bobby had been a few evenings before when Tinsley announced she would only need one of the Sisterhood for the night of the sixth. It was evident then that Bobby was to be her protégé. A leader among the Sisterhood.

"This way," she said quietly.

They followed the man through a narrow alleyway heavy with shadows. Bobby walked with caution, her eyes on Tinsley, who moved with her usual slow and deliberate grace. The music got louder as they approached the old warehouse. Guards at the entrance flashed a pink light at them. The man in the top hat announced himself, and the guards let them pass.

The space inside writhed with the masses of hundreds of people. As they crossed, a fight broke out. Through it all, Tinsley kept pace with them, as calm as ever. Several girls caught Bobby's eyes. They either waved or reached out to touch her as she passed. Her masculine dress openly displayed her preference. The air seemed charged with sexual energy, all generated by The Star, a local pop singer.

The Star danced on the main stage. She wore a dress that covered her breasts and genital area, but not much else. Her hair had been teased to an astounding height and adorned with glowing lights. She sang a raunchy song and moved in sync with her backup dancers. Bobby watched her stalk across the stage, her eyes intent on the audience below her.

A waitress passed by with a tray of drinks. Bobby was surprised to see Tinsley remove cash from her pocket and hand it to her.

"You do know these aren't your martinis," she shouted over the music. "This stuff is probably cut with battery acid."

Tinsley winked and nodded in reply. She turned her attention to the stage. Bobby gave the waitress the money and took two drinks from the tray. Bobby placed one drink in Tinsley's hands and watched her sip. Tinsley watched The Star dance onstage.

After the last song, The Star disappeared in a cloud of blue smoke. Bobby and Tinsley moved to the area behind the stage, crowded by fans hoping to be a part of The Star's court for the night. Top Hat guided them through to a door.

"I go first," Bobby told him. Tinsley handed her the bag and nodded.

Bobby pushed open the door and felt her heart quicken in her chest. The Star sat on a red cushioned chair, naked except for a very flimsy robe. An attendant was busy picking the lights from her hair. She still had the same presence she had onstage.

She sucked on a plastic tube, the other end attached to a lamp-like structure of clear glass that held a tempest of smoke.

"I was expecting an old man," she said.

"My employer is waiting outside," Bobby informed her. "She's very nervous about meeting you, about this place."

The Star raised her eyebrows. "She?"

"Yes," Bobby said, glancing around the room.

"And you are?"

"I watch over her."

She grinned in response. "Such a young thing. Seems you can barely watch over yourself."

Bobby stared at her openly for a moment, then remembered

the blue sack. She presented it to The Star and removed the bottle nestled inside.

"My employer wishes to gift you this," Bobby said. "It's tequila."

The Star laughed. "Real tequila?"

"Yes," Bobby said and handed over the bottle.

"Your employer must be rich," The Star said, taking it. "Such things are hard to come by. Glasses," she announced. "Three."

The attendant picking lights abandoned her task to bring a four-legged tray and three glasses. She left the room.

The Star was too preoccupied with the tequila to notice. She poured tequila into two of the glasses but hesitated at the third. "Your employer will be joining us?"

"Give her a minute or so," Bobby said. "She's very excited to meet you."

"Then sit and we will talk, you and I."

Bobby found a white iron chair and scooted it over. She sat.

"Drink," The Star insisted.

Bobby did. The Star downed one glass and poured another.

"That is real stuff."

"Yes," Bobby said. "The label on it was very interesting."

The Star finished up her second glass. "You are very lovely. What is your name?"

Bobby shifted in her seat and gave her name in a mumble.

The Star flashed a brilliant smile, let out a long, hearty chuckle, and poured herself another glass.

"So your employer, she gave my manager quite a bit of cash. She wants to fuck me?"

Bobby startled at her straightforwardness. "She hasn't told me."

The Star shrugged and caught hold of the neck of the bottle. Her wrists were slim and pale, like any other woman's. "What was so interesting about this label?"

"Your picture was on it, and it read Bacchanista."

She looked up at Bobby. "And this brought your employer to me?"

The door opened behind her. Bobby didn't have to turn to know that it was Tinsley. The Star's face went from cool apathy to alarm. She half stood in the chair and called out for someone named Tom.

"Calm yourself," Tinsley said in the old language.

The Star stopped screaming and sat angrily. "You. You're a fucking ghost."

"I'm very much alive, Leda."

"I'm The Star," she said indignantly.

Tinsley went up to her and reached out her hand. Leda took it and stood from the chair and into her embrace. She pulled away and asked sadly, "So you've come for me?"

Tinsley nodded gravely.

The Star walked away from her. "It took a while for the memories to come to me this time. I woke up in a drainage ditch with horrible dreams of beasts, and burning alive, and women in robes."

"I'm not here to hurt you," Tinsley said.

The Star chuckled bitterly. "Look at you. How fucking old are you?"

Tinsley grinned. "One hundred and twelve."

"And your Sandra?"

"She died some time ago. We had a full life together. We traveled the world. We ended up in what was once ancient Sumer. There we found the wisdom that would free you, no sacred fire, no way for the gates of the underworld to open."

The Star narrowed her eyes. "You lie to me."

"No, Leda," Tinsley said. "May I call you Leda?"

She nodded, still in disbelief. "You would free me?"

"I've devoted my life to it."

"What must I do?"

Tinsley motioned to the bottle. "You've already done it.

Mixed in with that tequila are the fabled waters of death. Now sleep."

At that, The Star collapsed to the floor. Tinsley dropped her cane to catch her. They both fell to the floor, Tinsley cradling the goddess in her lap. Bobby barred the door with a metal table.

She went to Tinsley and saw tears on her face. The goddess trembled in her arms. She spoke what Bobby knew to be the language of the Gods as her violet eyes melted into shimmering pools that dripped and then spilled from the corners of her eyes, over her ridiculous blue hair in twin rivulets that flowed across the floor and faded until they disappeared. Her lids fell over the empty cavities. She was gone.

Tinsley kissed her lips and looked up to Bobby. She reached out her hand. Bobby fetched the cane and helped her to her feet.

"Take me home," she said weakly. "Leave and do not return until morning. This is my last night in the world."

Bobby felt her entire body go numb. "You're tired—"

"No," Tinsley said sternly. "My time has come. The Sisterhood is yours to make what you will of it, Bobby."

Bobby nodded numbly and guided Tinsley out the other door and into an alley lit by garish red neon that made the wetness on the pavement look like blood. The car met them at the end.

"Tinsley is tired," Bobby said, trying to cover the emotion in her voice. "Let's get her home quickly so that she can rest."

They said nothing until the car coasted past the gates of Tinsley's home. The old church. It was fitting she would want to die there in the home where she shared so many years with her beloved Sandra. Together, they had traveled the world seeking out the ancient myths and finding the waters of death. Along the way, they found enough mysteries to keep the Sisterhood busy for many years to come.

"I'll go alone," she said when Bobby tried to follow. She clasped Bobby's hand, and the sudden strength nearly took Bobby's breath away.

"What you have admired in me for so long is now yours to protect," she said and went inside.

Bobby wished she could say something but found she could not. She watched Tinsley go inside and told the driver to take her back to the hotel. There would be much planning to do, in a little time. Tomorrow would come the seventh day of the seventh month of the seventh year.

About the Author

Tanai started writing strange little novels at the age of fourteen and dreamed of becoming a published author. She is a hard-core musicphile and enjoys everything from bluegrass to rap to metal. She has an extensive collection of digital music files, CDs, and vinyl. She lives with her hilarious, wonderful girlfriend, Janette, and their three dogs, Zeus, Zoey, and Beto.

Books Available From Bold Strokes Books

Switchblade by Carsen Taite. Lines were meant to be crossed. Third in the Luca Bennett Bounty Hunter Series. (978-1-62639-058-4)

Nightingale by Andrea Bramhall. Culture, faith, and duty conspire to tear two young lovers apart, yet fate seems to have different plans for them both. (978-1-62639-059-1)

No Boundaries by Donna K. Ford. A chance meeting and a nightmare from the past threaten more than Andi Massey's solitude as she and Gwen Palmer struggle to understand the complexity of love without boundaries. (978-1-62639-060-7)

Sacred Fire by Tanai Walker. Tinsley Swann is cursed to change into a beast for seven days every seven years. When she meets Leda, she comes face-to-face with her past. (978-1-62639-061-4)

Timeless by Rachel Spangler. When Stevie Geller returns to her hometown, will she do things differently the second time around or will she be in such a hurry to leave her past that she misses out on a better future? (978-1-62639-050-8)

Second to None by L.T. Marie. Can a physical therapist and a custom motorcycle designer conquer their pasts and build a future with one another? (978-1-62639-051-5)

Seneca Falls by Jesse Thoma. Together, two women discover love truly can conquer all evil. (978-1-62639-052-2)

A Kingdom Lost by Barbara Ann Wright. Without knowing each other's fates, Princess Katya and her consort Starbride seek to reclaim their kingdom from the magic-wielding madman who seized the throne and is murdering their people. (978-1-62639-053-9)

Season of the Wolf by Robin Summers. Two women running from their pasts are thrust together by an unimaginable evil. Can they overcome the horrors that haunt them in time to save each other? (978-1-62639-043-0)

The Heat of Angels by Lisa Girolami. Fires burn in more than one place in Los Angeles. (978-1-62639-042-3)

Desperate Measures by P. J. Trebelhorn. Homicide detective Kay Griffith and contractor Brenda Jansen meet amidst turmoil neither of them is aware of until murder suspect Tommy Rayne makes his move to exact revenge on Kay. (978-1-62639-044-7)

The Magic Hunt by L.L. Raand. With her Pack being hunted by human extremists and beset by enemies masquerading as friends, can Sylvan protect them and her mate, or will she succumb to the feral rage that threatens to turn her rogue, destroying them all? A Midnight Hunters novel. (978-1-62639-045-4)

Wingspan by Karis Walsh. Wildlife biologist Bailey Chase is content to live at the wild bird sanctuary she has created on Washington's Olympic Peninsula until she is lured beyond the safety of isolation by architect Kendall Pearson. (978-1-60282-983-1)

Night Bound by Winter Pennington. Kass struggles to keep her head, her heart, and her relationships in order. She's still having a difficult time accepting being an Alpha female—but her wolf is certain of what she wants and she's intent on securing her power. (978-1-60282-984-8)

The Blush Factor by Gun Brooke. Ice-cold business tycoon Eleanor Ashcroft only cares about the three Ps—Power, Profit, and Prosperity—until young Addison Garr makes her doubt both that and the state of her frostbitten heart. (978-1-60282-985-5)

Slash and Burn by Valerie Bronwen. The murder of a roundly despised author at an LGBT writers' conference in New Orleans turns Winter Lovelace's relaxing weekend hobnobbing with her peers into a nightmare of suspense—especially when her ex turns up. (978-1-60282-986-2)

The Quickening: A Sisters of Spirits novel by Yvonne Heidt. Ghosts, visions, and demons are all in a day's work for Tiffany. But when Kat asks for help on a serial killer case, life takes on another dimension altogether. (978-1-60282-975-6)